1

"A mind is a terrible thing to waste"

Arthur Fletcher

"The line between good and evil is permeable and almost anyone can be induced to cross it when pressured by situational forces."

Phillip Zimbardo

Pine View Institute

© 2022

P.S. Winn

"Not until we are lost, do we begin to understand ourselves."
                          Henry David Thoreau

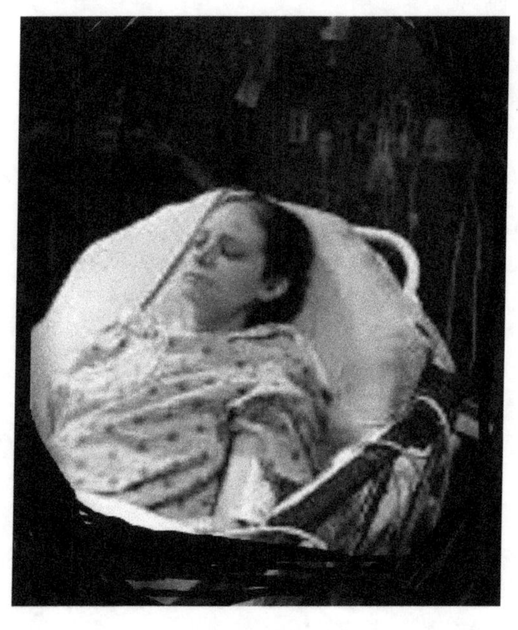

Chapter 1

Opening slowly, the light brown eyes squinted with confusion. Slowly moving from side to side, the woman knew something was wrong. She knew she was on a bed, but not much else.
A sliver of light from a door on the far side of the room, barely illuminated the area. The woman could almost hear the sound of her rapidly beating heart. Taking in slow breaths, she was able to get her heart rate slightly under control. Her mind was reeling.
"Where was she? How did she get here?"
As another thought hit her like a lightning strike on a stormy day, her heart took off again.
"Who am I?"
The light brown eyes widened. One hand lifted, followed by the other. She grabbed her hair in a tight grip. The words floating in her mind had her nerves jumping.
"Think, damn it, think."
Hands moved from the grip on her hair to cover her eyes. She felt like crying, maybe screaming. Not knowing where she was, the woman didn't want the latter to happen. Eyes still covered, she shook her head and berated herself.
"Come on Kelly, you can do this."
Removing her hands from her eyes, the woman sighed with relief.
"Kelly, my name is Kelly."
Now, she wondered what last name might go with the first. She tried to concentrate and think, but no

further resolution came to her. She would have to accept the one name title, for now.

Trying to raise herself to a sitting position, Kelly instead, collapsed back onto the slim pillow, as a wave of dizziness hit her. She closed her eyes and tried to remain calm. She looked down at her body, seeing she wore some type of loose pajamas. She didn't recognize them. Then again, she didn't have a remembrance of much right now. She knew her name was Kelly, but nothing else came to her mind. She couldn't remember, not only her last name, but where she might be from. Again questions ran through her mind, fast, furious, and fearful.

"Do I have a family? Am I in danger? What the hell is happening? How do I figure this out?"

Once again, the slow, deep breaths began. She had to relax. Freaking out wasn't going to solve anything.

The sound of the door, standing not far from the one with the thin light, opening, had Kelly turning her head. The light from the hallway, lifted the shadows in the room somewhat. Kelly stared, as a woman in a white uniform, stepped into the room.

Moving toward the bed, the woman stared at Kelly. "You're awake. I wasn't expecting that so soon."

To Kelly, the words sounded like an accusation. Almost a reprimand for her being awake. Kelly could only stare. She had no way to know if the woman in white was friend or foe.

Moving to the door, that was only partially opened, the woman pushed it inward. More light spilled into the room. Kelly could now see that door led to a bathroom. Moving from the doorway leading to the bathroom, the woman moved closer to the bed. Reaching in her uniform, she pulled something from her pocket. Leaning over, she ran the thing across Kelly's forehead.
Looking at the device, the woman nodded.
"Good, your temperature is normal."

Frowning, Kelly licked her dry lips. Although afraid, she had to speak. She needed answers.
"Where am I?"
Her quiet voice, cracked with the three words.

Staring at Kelly, the woman's eyes narrowed. For a moment, Kelly thought she saw hatred as the brown eyes narrowed. The woman smiled slightly, and her expression changed. Kelly thought her mind must have been imagining things.
Drawing in a breath, the woman nodded at Kelly.
"You're at the Pine View Institute. You were in a car wreck. You should consider yourself lucky. Pine View is well known as one of the best trauma care centers in the country."
The smile grew larger, like the woman was taking credit for the achievement she had mentioned.

Kelly frowned. "I don't remember that."
She was relieved her voice sounded stronger now, more steady.

The woman nodded at Kelly.
"You may have some problems with your memory. You did sustain head injuries. I'll go find the doctor. He can explain better than I can."

Kelly frowned. "Who are you?"

The woman shook her head. Her rust colored hair was pulled back in a tight ponytail.
"That should have been my first comment. My name is Barbara Adams. I'm the head nurse on the Pinyon Unit."
The nurse frowned.
"Can you tell me your name?"

Staring at the woman, Kelly frowned.
"My name is Kelly."

Nurse Adams nodded.
"Okay, that's good. You just rest now, I'll notify the doctor. He will be in soon."
That said, the nurse hurried out of the room, leaving Kelly more confused than ever.

Closing her eyes, Kelly tried to focus her mind and her memory. Being in a car accident might be reason enough for her confusion, but that excuse didn't feel right to her. Her body didn't feel sore. Lifting her arms, Kelly studied them, looking for any signs of cuts or bruising and saw none. She did see a small, round mark on the inside of her elbow and wondered

what might have caused that. What she really wanted
to do, was get out of the bed, and go look in the
adjoined bathroom, to see if there might be a mirror.
She had remembered her first name, but she had no
inkling of who she was or what she looked like. The
nurse had said the doctor would be in to see her.
Kelly didn't want to be out of her bed when that
happened. She didn't know why, but she felt it was
best to stay where she was until after the doctor's
visit. Kelly wasn't even sure she could make it the
short distance to the bathroom. She'd gotten dizzy
just trying to sit up. Still, she knew, once she was left
alone, that is exactly what she would be doing, even
if she had to crawl. Shaking her head slightly, Kelly
felt the beginnings of a headache. She closed her
eyes, trying to wish that pain away.
The door opened again and Kelly's eyes opened. She
had no idea how long it had been since the nurse had
left. She didn't think she had fallen asleep, but
wasn't sure. She wished the room had a clock, but
glancing around she saw none. What she did see,
was an older man stepping in the room. The nurse
she met earlier followed close behind.
The man had on a white jacket. His gray streaked,
light brown hair was combed perfectly. He stared at
Kelly with dark blue eyes. She thought the look held
anger, but wasn't positive.

The man took a couple steps in the room. Grabbing a
chair, he placed it a foot away from the bed. He
carried a clipboard and a pen.

"Nurse Adams informed me you were awake. That is
indeed good news. I'm Doctor Joseph Mengle. I am
the lead doctor here at the institute. Nurse Adams
tells me she informed you that you were in an
accident."
The doctor looked down at his clipboard for a
moment before looking back at Kelly.
"I think we should start with a few simple questions.
Can you tell me your name?"

Nodding, Kelly felt the pangs of the headache again.
"Kelly, my name is Kelly."

The doctor frowned. "Do you have a last name to
add to that?"

Although earlier she couldn't think of her full name,
now she blurted it out without even thinking.
"Mitchell. My name is Kelly Mitchell."

Again the doctor nodded.
"You're doing well Miss Mitchell. Now, could you
tell me your address?"

Mind whirling, Kelly tried to think, but came up
blank. She frowned, staring at the doctor. The sound
of him, clicking his pen over and over, was messing
with her concentration.
"I can't remember that right now. To tell you the
truth, I think I'm a bit foggy from sleeping. How
long have I been here?"

The doctor's smile didn't touch his eyes.
"You've been at the Institute just over a week."

Brown eyes widened.
"Have I been asleep all that time?"

The doctor nodded, his pen seemed to click faster.
"Yes, tonight is the first time you have been awake.
In fact, you should still be resting. You suffered
quite a lot of brain trauma. The best thing for you
right now is to get rest."

A sigh escaped. The last thing she wanted to do was
rest. Kelly glanced at the nurse, then turned to stare
at the doctor.
"What time is it?"
She noticed the doctor didn't have on a watch.

Still he answered quickly.
"It's just after midnight. I'm going to leave and let
you rest. In the morning, either I, or my associate,
Doctor Anders, will be in to check on you."
The doctor stood.
"Again, it is good to see you awake. Nurse Adams
will be taking care of you the remainder of the night.
I want you to stay in bed. Head traumas can have
lasting damage, until we know the extent, it is best to
take it easy."
He turned to the nurse.
"I'll leave Miss Mitchell in your hands."
That said, the doctor walked out the door.

Kelly noticed the man had called her 'Miss'. She wondered if that meant she wasn't married or if it had just been an unrelated use of the word.
After the doctor left the room, Kelly looked at the nurse.
"Does my family know I am here?"
She asked the question without knowing with any kind of certainty if she had family members who might be worried about her.

Nurse Adams shook her head.
"We had no idea who to notify. We didn't even know your true name until just now. When you were brought here, you had no identification or any personal belongings. I'm sure Doctor Mengle will look into all your information now that you have shared your name. It would have been helpful for you to recall your address, but he will at least have something to go on now."

Listening to the nurse, Kelly felt certain the woman was lying. She couldn't explain the feeling, but it was there, none the less.

Reaching in her pocket, the nurse pulled out a medicine bottle. Walking to the table next to Kelly's bed, she grabbed a cup and filled it from a small pitcher. She held out the cup and removed one pill from the bottle.
"You need to take your medication."

Kelly frowned. "What is that?"

The grin on Nurse Adams' face didn't look genuine to Kelly. She stepped closer.
"It's a muscle relaxer. The doctor ordered it for you. It will keep you calm and help you rest."

Kelly shook her head, trying to ignore the pain.
"I don't want to take that. The doctor said I've been asleep over a week. Isn't that enough?"

Again, the fake smile appeared.
"The doctor knows what is best. I can always get his permission to put in an IV and administer your medication that way."

Horror set in, as Kelly realized the nurse meant what she said. She reluctantly took the pill. Trying to sit up, Kelly shook her head.
"I can't swallow this from my position."

A look of disgust came and went quickly, as Nurse Adams reached down and pushed a button that raised the head of Kelly's bed. Once Kelly was in a sitting position, the nurse handed her the small cup she held.
"There, that's better. Just take your medicine and you'll feel much better."

Taking the cup, Kelly slipped the pill in her mouth and took a sip of the water, which was half warm. She could see nurse Adams watching her. Apparently making sure the medicine was taken.

Kelly grimaced, and then tried to hide the motion with a grin. She handed the cup back.
"I think I need to use the bathroom."

Nurse Adams shook her head.
"Feeling like you have to urinate is normal. You have a catheter in. We had to do that while you were sleeping. With you awake now, I'll check with the doctor about removing it. I get off shift at seven a.m. If I don't remove it by then, I'll talk to nurse Parker when our shifts change. Until then, you should be sleeping anyway."

Looking around the room, Kelly frowned.
"I'm really not tired. I mean, I have been sleeping for days. Isn't there a television in here somewhere? I don't see one."

Nurse Adams shook her head.
"We don't allow televisions on the Pinyon Unit. With head traumas, we find too much stimulation, hinders the recovery progress. Now, I really need to get going. You aren't my only patient on this floor. The best thing you can do, is get some rest. In the morning, we can worry about making some changes."

Turning, Nurse Adams left the room, closing the door that led to the hallway behind her.
Kelly was grateful the bathroom door was left wide open allowing the light into the room. She looked

around now, trying to orient herself to the space she was in.

The curtains, which Kelly assumed, covered a window, were shut. A small door, in the corner, looked like it was a closet. Kelly wanted to get up and check, but wasn't sure if she could move with the catheter, the nurse spoke of, still in place. She had no memory if she ever had a catheter before or not. That left her with no idea what the device entailed or how it would hamper her movement. Frustration and anger combined to overwhelm her. Tears slid down her face. Reaching up, Kelly wiped them away and resolved to not let that happen again. She needed to find out what was happening. Between the nurse and the doctor, Kelly was left with a feeling that something wasn't quite right about this strange place she found herself in.

She could feel her eyes growing heavy and wondered just how strong the medication was she had been given.

Chapter 2

The sound of someone humming, woke Kelly.

Opening her eyes, expecting to see the nurse from the night before, Kelly stared at the new person in her room. The smile the woman gave her, seemed a bit warmer, than the one she had gotten from Nurse Adams.

The blonde haired woman, looked at Kelly with cornflower blue eyes.
"Well, good morning. I heard you had awoken last night, but until now, I wasn't sure that was true. Seeing is believing. I'm your nurse today. I'm Susan Parker. How are you feeling?"

Frowning at the question, Kelly didn't have an answer to yet, she shrugged.
"Right now, I feel like I need to use the bathroom. I know Nurse Adams said I had a catheter, but I really think I need to go. I'd hate to have an accident here in the bed."

The woman nodded. "You may have to go, I removed your catheter when I got on shift at seven. Let me help you get up. You've been in that bed for days. You might feel dizzy and a bit weak. If you start feeling weakness, just make sure to make me aware of it. Believe me, it is easier to prop you up than to pick you up."

Nodding at the nurse, Kelly sighed. To her it
sounded like the nurse having to pick her up was a
bother she didn't want to deal with. Ignoring the
feeling, Kelly nodded.
"Thanks for the warning. I think I better try to get to
that bathroom."

Nurse Parker stepped over to Kelly's bed and took
her arm. She slowly helped Kelly sit up and move so
she was seated on the edge of her bed. Even that
slow movement did cause the room to feel like it was
tilting slightly. Closing her eyes, Kelly waited a
moment, then opened them. A grin appeared when
the room once again felt normal. She sighed.
"Okay, I think I'm ready to try standing."

Moving a bit closer, the nurse slid an arm around
Kelly's waist.
"Go ahead and stand up. We;ll go slow. Just let me
know if you get too dizzy or feel nauseous.

Nodding, Kelly didn't speak, saving her energy for
the short journey to the bathroom. It took several
minutes, but the two made it to the door.
Susan stared at Kelly.
"Do you want me to go in and help you in there? It
might be for the best. Like I said, we don't want you
falling."

Thinking of the woman helping her use the bathroom,
Kelly shook her head in repulsion. The last thing she

wanted was someone she didn't know, let alone trust, come in with her while she used the bathroom.
"I think I can do this. I promise to call out if I have problems."

Although Kelly could see the nurse wasn't happy with her answer, Susan gave her a slight nod.
"I'll be standing just outside this door."

Moving away from Nurse Parker, Kelly made her way into the bathroom. She shut the door behind her, wishing it had a lock of some kind. Kelly couldn't remember much, but she had a feeling she was shy when it came to personal hygiene.
Instead of walking to use the toilet, Kelly stepped over to a mirror above a small sink. It was only a couple of steps. The room was small, with only a shower, a toilet and sink. There were no cabinets of any kind. The freestanding sink didn't even have one. Staring in the mirror, Kelly's hopes fell. She had thought seeing her reflection would bring back memories. Looking at her face in the mirror, Kelly guessed her age to be somewhere in her early thirties. Light brown eyes stared back at her. Kelly could see dark circles underneath. She ran a hand through her short, dark brown hair. It looked like it needed a good washing or at the very least, a comb run through it. Kelly noticed one side of her mouth was slightly crooked. She smiled at herself and saw her smile matched the crooked line. She shrugged, not really caring about the dissimilarity. Her face was pale. Kelly guessed that was normal. She was in a

hospital after all. She wasn't sure if she would be called attractive, but could imagine the word 'cute' being used in association with the reflection she was staring at. What Kelly didn't see, was any damage from being in an accident.
Turning away from the mirror, Kelly hurried over and used the toilet. Once finished, she headed back to the sink. Kelly washed her hands before opening the door again.

Like she had stated, Susan was standing outside the door. If Kelly would have taken one more step when she opened the door, she would have ran into the nurse. Reaching out, Susan took Kelly's arm.
"I was just about to come in after you. I thought you might have fainted."

Trying too give the nurse a grin, Kelly shrugged.
"I'm okay. I didn't even get dizzy in there."
Then she frowned and let out a sigh.
"Is there a comb around here I could use? My hair's a mess."

Susan nodded. "Why don't we get you back over to the bed first? I'll grab some hygiene stuff for you. There's a patient packet in the closet."

Back on the bed, raised to a sitting position, Kelly watched Nurse Parker go to the closet and grab a plastic square pan.

Watching her, Kelly wondered if she had any personal items sitting in that closet, but didn't ask the question.

The nurse placed the pan on Kelly's lap.

Looking in, Kelly saw a comb, toothbrush, toothpaste, mouthwash and deodorant. All the items were in small packages.

Looking up at Nurse Parker, Kelly grinned.

"Thanks, I can use this stuff."

Susan nodded. "Just don't try going alone to the bathroom to use them. If I'm not here, you can push the button on the side of your bed and I'll come running."

Susan frowned. "In fact, right now, I need to go. Doctor Mengle usually leaves at seven when Doctor Anders comes in. I know Doctor Mengle wanted to see you before he left. I'll go and let him know you're awake. I'll also bring back your breakfast tray with me. I imagine you're hungry."

Looking at the woman, Kelly thought about what she had said. The truth was, she wasn't hungry. That didn't seem possible, if she had been sleeping for a week or so. Then she thought about the mark on the inside of her arm. Was it from an IV? Kelly blinked her eyes amazed that she knew what an IV was, but couldn't remember anything about her past. She was hopeful her remembering anything might mean the other lost memories would return. Kelly shrugged.

"I guess I could manage to eat."

After the nurse left the room, Kelly pulled the comb
from the pan and ran it through her hair. She ran her
tongue along the front of her teeth and wished she
could head back to the bathroom and brush them.
Instead she took the pan, with its' contents and set
the whole thing on the table by her bed. The item she
had placed the pan on wasn't much of a table. It was
on wheels and only had a top with one small drawer.
Kelly thought the thing was made to slide over her
lap as she sat up on the bed. She pulled open the
drawer, to only find it was empty.
Now that the room light was on, Kelly looked
around. The walls were a tan color. Nothing adorned
them. No clock, no pictures, just the plain looking,
super light brown walls. She could only see one
curtain in the room and it was drawn closed. Also tan,
the window covering was a shade darker than the
walls. Kelly wondered what she would see, if she got
up and looked out? She decided to wait until after
Doctor Mengle made his visit and no nurses were
around. For some reason, she felt her snooping might
not be welcome. She glanced over at the door where
Nurse Parker had gotten her the pan of hygiene items
Kelly wondered if that closet held anything else.
Maybe something that belonged to her. Some
personal item that would trigger her lost memories.
She didn't have time to wonder for long, as the door
to her room opened, and the doctor, who had talked
to her the night before, stepped in.

Like the previous night, the first thing Kelly noticed
was the man looked immaculate. His short gray

streaked, light brown hair, was combed neatly and his white jacket looked like someone had just run an iron over it. The dark blue eyes stared at her.
"Good morning Miss Mitchell. Nurse Parker tells me you were able to take a short walk this morning. I know it was just a few steps, but that is very encouraging."

Although the greeting seemed to be friendly, Kelly noticed the words were spoken in a monotone voice. Still, she nodded and gave the man a grin.
"Yes, I was a bit dizzy at first, but that has passed."

The doctor nodded.
"That's good to hear. I'm going off shift right now, but Doctor Anders will be in to check on you later. I just wanted to let you know we are working on finding out if you have some relatives we can notify of your condition."

Kelly sighed. "What is my condition? I don't seem to have any cuts or bruises. I don't feel any pain like I've been in a car accident. My memory is a bit cloudy, but nothing else feels wrong."

The doctor laughed, a bit harshly.
"Now Miss Mitchell, I am the doctor here. The problem with your memory may be more serious than you think. We have to do more testing to know for sure. I hope you understand, we just have your best interest in mind. While we take time to search

for your relatives, you just need to rest and get better."

The door to the room opened again and Susan Parker stuck her head in.
"Sorry to interrupt Doctor Mengle. I have Kelly's breakfast. I can come back if you're busy."

The man shook his head.
"No, I'm finished here. In fact, my shift ended hours ago. I should already be home."
He turned back to Kelly.
"Just rest for now. I come back on shift tonight."
Without saying anything else the doctor left the room.

Bringing in a tray, Susan placed it on the table. She moved the table so it sat over the bed and covered Kelly's lap. Susan pointed at the tray.
"Scrambled eggs, toast, coffee and orange juice for breakfast. It's a light meal until your stomach gets used to having actual food again. I'll be back in about an hour to pick up the tray. You should easily be finished by then."

Kelly only nodded, then watched the nurse leave, closing the door shut behind her.
As soon as nurse Parker was gone, Kelly pushed the table back. and sat on the edge of the bed. The food could wait. Right now, Kelly knew she only had a short time to investigate.

Standing from the bed, the first thing she did was head to the curtained window. Pulling one corner back, Kelly looked out the window. She stared in disbelief. The first thought that came to mind was, she thought the institute had picked a perfect name. All she could see was a view of the pines. Most of the branches were so thick she couldn't see past them. Although Kelly knew nothing about the building she found herself in, she realized she wasn't on the bottom floor. Many of the tree tops were taller than her vantage point allowed her to see. She could look down and see the trunks though. She had been told it was morning. If that was true, she knew she had to be looking to the west. The direction the shadows fell, meant the rising sun had to be on the opposite side of the building.

The forest, that seemed to go on forever, wasn't a place she wanted to explore if she ever got out of the institute. Kelly hoped the front of the building had a clear road to wherever her home might be.

Closing the curtain, Kelly felt as lost as she had before she had looked out.

Turning toward the closet door, Kelly opened it slowly. She hoped to find something to trigger her memory, but feared looking would only make her anxious with frustration. Still, she had to look.

Staring in the small area, she saw an empty metal bar running from side to side at the top of the closet. No hangers, no clothes. She sighed as her eyes dropped to the bottom floor of the space. She stared at a pair of tennis shoes. Kneeling down, she frowned.

The shoes didn't look familiar. Reaching out, she lifted the pair. The spot beneath where the shoes had been sitting, was bare, except for a couple of pine needles, and a few specks of dirt. Turning the shoes over, she examined the bottoms. Kelly's frown deepened, seeing the tracks on the bottoms of the shoes were free of debris. The soles looked like someone had cleaned them.

She placed the shoes back, trying to put them in the exact spot they had been pulled from. As she carefully set the shoes down, her mind reeled into a flashback.

Kelly could see herself. She sat in a chair, holding a shoebox, wrapped in what looked like birthday style paper. Tearing off the paper, Kelly saw the same shoes she had just been studying. Lifting them out of the box, a large smile covered her face. She turned to look at a woman standing near her.

Before Kelly saw more, the flashback disappeared. She let out a sorrowful groan. Although she hadn't had enough of a glimpse into the past to know who the woman was, she had seen the similarities.

The woman in her vision looked like an older version of the image Kelly had seen in the mirror earlier. The resemblance was strong enough, Kelly knew the person she had just seen, was a relative. Maybe her mother, or an aunt. The person was enough older, Kelly didn't think she was a sister. She had darker hair than Kelly. The thick strands, also longer, hung to the woman's shoulders.

Dumbfounded by her revelation, Kelly stood in shock for what felt like an eternity.

Finally, she shook her head. Kelly had no idea how long she had been away from her bed. Nurse Parker had said she'd be back to get the food tray. The last thing Kelly wanted, was for anyone to find she had been up, and snooping around.
Heading back toward the bed, Kelly stared at the door to her room. She wanted to check out one more thing. She drew in a breath, hoping she still had enough time.
Moving to the door, Kelly reached down and grabbed the knob. She wanted to get a glimpse at what might be outside.Turning the knob, Kelly frowned angrily. The door was locked.
Her mind whirled. Why in the world would her door be locked? Kelly had no answer to that question. She also knew in her heart, if she asked, she wouldn't be told the truth.

She hurried back to the bed, thankful no one had opened her door before she got back in place.

Chapter 3

At the same time Kelly was doing her small bit of exploring, Doctor Mengle was in Doctor Anders office. He had taken off his white coat and put his clipboard and pen away. Seated in a chair, he looked around the room, before looking across the desk at the only other person in the room.
Doctor Mengle had placed Doctor Anders in the office, mostly because it was smaller than his own. He was the man in charge, and wanted to make sure everyone was aware of that fact. Mengle frowned, looking at Anders' cluttered desk. He would never allow the desk in his office to be in that condition. Joseph had a touch of a compulsion disorder, but brushed it off as a doctor wanting to look professional.

Doctor Anders, was younger than Doctor Mengle. His blonde hair, longer than Mengle's own, touched his collar. His brown eyes were frowning, wondering just why his boss had asked for a conference.
He watched the dark blue eyes, across from him, narrow.
"Phil, I know I usually don't tell you how to care for the subjects. I feel like I needed to warn you about Miss Mitchell, though. She's fully awake now.
Susan tells me that, although Miss Mitchell took her medication, she wasn't all that willing. I think it would be in our best interest to keep a closer eye on her. I don't want any slip-ups with her."

A frown crossed Phil's brow.

"Damn it Joseph, I hate when you call the people here subjects. They're patients. As I doctor, I feel it is our best interest, and theirs, to at least give them an inkling of respect."

Phil drew in a breath and let it out slowly.

"We made the decision to take away the medication, and allow Kelly Mitchell to wake. She was under much longer than the others. I'll watch her, mostly for that reason, but I'm sure there's no problem. If anything, problems would be caused by the long, induced coma we had her in."

The blue eyes darkened further, making Phil wonder if he'd gone too far. He knew better than to antagonize his boss. Joseph Mengle was the institute's director. He had been one of the founding members of Pine View.

Phil didn't have a problem giving Kelly special attention. The institute didn't have many patients to watch over. The four units held only seven patients each, right now. The units, named after the trees, associated with the institute's name, sat with two on each floor of the building. The top floor, where Kelly was a patient, held the Pinyon and Spruce floors. The main level consisted of the Conifer and Ponderosa units. Each unit was specifically designed for different types of patients. On the two units on the top floor, the patients were more coherent. A few, on the bottom units, were almost totally incapacitated. Phil wasn't even sure how some remained alive or what strange experiments Doctor Mengle did on

them. The downstairs, Conifer Unit, was Mengle's
domain.
Phil actually, was happy for that.

Across from Phil, Joseph had reached forward to pull
a pen from the holder on Phil's desk.
Staring at the man, Phil tried not to cringe, as Joseph
began clicking the pen. Phil hadn't decided if the
man had a nervous tic, or just clicked the pen,
knowing it annoyed others.
Either way, Phil hated the sound.

Joseph was shaking his head. His blue eyes, were
dark with hatred.
"Patients, subjects, whatever you want to call them,
doesn't really matter. I'm just asking you to keep an
eye on Miss Mitchell. I assume you can do that."

Trying not to cringe at the harsh sound of Joseph's
voice, Phil sighed.
"Yes, I can do that. Listen, I appreciate the heads up.
I'll make sure to check on her a few extra times
during my shift."
A frown appeared, making Phil look older than his
thirty two years.
"Does she have any memories back yet?"
Phil could have looked in Kelly's chart, but wanted
to hear first hand, what the doctor might have found
out. Although, Phil didn't really like his boss, he had
to admit, Mengle was good at what he did.

Doctor Mengle shook his head, and smiled. The grin, didn't touch his eyes and looked menacing.
"She knows her name and that's about it. She is asking questions though. I don't like that."

Now Phil shrugged, thinking who wouldn't ask questions and want some answers. He couldn't imagine what it would be like to wake in a strange place with no memories of how you got there, or worse, anything about your past.
"Does she know she was in, what we are calling, an accident?"

Nodding, Mengle's face still held the smile, which to Phil, still looked more like a grimace.
"I made sure to tell her that. I'm not sure if she believed the story, but there's really no way for her to discount what I said."
Mengle stood and glared down at Phil.
"Just make sure things stay that way. I have a feeling Miss Mitchell may be a valuable subject."
Leaving the last word he said, the one Phil didn't like, hanging in the air, Joseph Mengle strode out of the room.

Chapter 4

Kelly had been back in her place on the bed about twenty minutes when the door opened. The door, Kelly now knew, was kept locked from the outside.

Susan Parker stepped into the room, closing the door behind her. She looked over at Kelly and started to smile. She stopped, and frowned instead, seeing the tray of food.
"You didn't eat anything I brought you. I thought you'd be hungry."

A shrug, was followed by her own frown.
"I'm sorry, I guess I wasn't hungry. I did try to drink some of that coffee, but I must like sugar. It tasted a bit bitter to me."

Moving to the bed, Susan shrugged.
"I guess we can try again at lunch."
She held out her hand with a pill in it.
"Doctor Mengle prescribed this before he left this morning."

Kelly frowned. "I don't want any more sleeping or anxiety pills. I don't need those or muscle relaxers. I've slept too much."

Shaking her head, Susan still held out the pill.
"This isn't either of those things. It's just an antibiotic. With you having that catheter in for so

long, we don't want you to get an infection. This is for your own good. Why don't you wash it down with that orange juice? Some vitamin C couldn't hurt."

Taking the pill, Kelly gave Susan a disgusted look. "I'd rather go out in the sunshine for vitamin C. I guess if this is an antibiotic, it's okay to take."
Then she frowned.
"If you have no records on me, what happens if I'm allergic to the medicines you are making me take?"

Susan grunted and shook her head.
"I am a nurse and you are watched over by doctors. We know how to handle things like that here at the institute."
Susan watched closely, as Kelly put the pill in her mouth, grabbed her juice and washed it down.
Kelly would have liked to spit the pill out, but felt the scrutiny she was under, meant that wasn't a good idea.

Once the pill was taken, Susan picked up the food tray. Now, she smiled at Kelly.
"I'll just get this out of your way. I'm not sure what time Doctor Anders will be in, but I'm sure it will be after lunch. He usually starts his day with the patients downstairs."

Wishing she didn't have to talk with any doctors, especially another like Doctor Mengle, Kelly frowned.

"I've already had the visit from Doctor Mengle. What I'd really like, is something to do. This room doesn't have a television. Do you have a magazine or a book I could read?"

Susan shrugged. "I'll ask the doctor about that. I know both the doctors here, frown on too much stimulation after a head injury."

Disgusted by the answer, Kelly only shrugged, figuring nothing she said would make a difference.

Picking up the tray, Susan stared at Kelly with a small amount of compassion.
"I know it's hard just sitting in this room. I promise to ask about some reading material for you. I better get this tray down to the kitchen. I'll be back later with your lunch."

Heading to the door, Susan opened it without a problem. Kelly figured the nurse must have left the thing unlocked, just for the time she was in the room. Kelly was certain once Nurse Parker left, the door would once again be locked up tight.

After she was once again alone, Kelly shook her head at the dilemma she was in. If she had truly been in an accident and had head trauma, why wasn't she getting treatment for that? So far, all she knew was there was something strange about the institute.

Even both Nurse Adams, and Nurse Parker,
repeating the idea that watching TV was too much
stimulus, seemed ridiculous to Kelly.
She sighed and leaned back on her pillow. Kelly was
still sitting up, afraid if she lowered the head of the
bed, she would fall asleep.

A half an hour later, Kelly frowned and sat up
straighter.
Something was wrong.
The room seemed to grow dark, despite the lights
being on. For no reason, Kelly suddenly felt
depressed. Not the dispirited feeling she had, being
in the institute, this feeling, was one of despondence.
She stared around and the room seemed to change.
Kelly wondered if Nurse Parker had lied about the
pill she had given her.
Kelly's hand went to her chest as her heart sped up.
Darkness seemed to press in on her.
Suddenly, instead of the shadows she was seeing,
Kelly watched as colored lights seemed to appear all
around her, distorting her vision. She could no
longer see the room, despite the shadows leaving.
The sound of a voice came to her. That too, seemed
distorted.

"It's okay Kelly. Just come with me. I can help you."

A deep frowned slashed across Kelly's forehead.
"Who are you? I can't see you. What's happening?"

The voice, which Kelly decided was definitely male, continued speaking. She felt a hand on her shoulder. "You need to come with me. I can fix what's happening. Trust me Kelly."

Not knowing who, or what, to trust, Kelly did as she was told. Slipping her legs over the side of the bed, she stood and followed the man.
In her confused state, Kelly wasn't sure if she had walked two steps, or two miles, before she was helped to a chair.
Sitting down, Kelly clenched the narrow arms of the chair. Her heart was still racing as the disembodied voice spoke again.

"Take a deep breath. Slowly, breath in and out. Good, you're doing fine Kelly. I'm going to think of an object. I need you to tell me what I am thinking of."

Again, the frown formed. The light brown eyes narrowed.
"I don't know what you're talking about. Who are you? Where am I?"

The sound of the voice seemed to reverberate in Kelly's head.
"None of that matters, just focus your mind Kelly. What am I thinking of?"

Fear hit Kelly like a load of bricks being dropped on her. She had no idea what was happening. She still could only see the dazzling display of lights flashing

in her vision and nothing else. Then, suddenly, she saw something else. She frowned.
"A football, I see a football."

The voice answered with a lighter tone. To Kelly it sounded like the man was pleased.
"Good Kelly, very good. Now what?"

Again the frown, before Kelly nodded.
"A cat. I see a gray cat."

"Now what?"

The pictures were flashing in Kelly's mind now. To her, it seemed as if someone was flashing cards with pictures on them.
"An elephant, a car, a road, no wait, it's more like a path. Now I see a clown, a kitchen stove, a snake." Kelly frowned now, the scene in front of her was no longer like a flash card. It was more like watching a short scene from a movie.
"A murder, oh my God, no. Please stop. He's killing her, make him stop."
Kelly watched in horror as a man, dressed all in black, with a ski mask on, slashed the throat of a young woman.
Her hands went up to cover her eyes, trying to stop the moving picture in front of her. The scene continued, even with her eyes closed, and covered.
"Please, no more. I don't want to see this."

The sight she was seeing, was replaced by the bright, flashing lights once again.

Kelly sighed. The lights were bothering her, but were much better than the atrocity she had just witnessed.

Once again, she felt a hand on her shoulder.
"You did fine Kelly. Stand up, I'll get you back to the safety of your room. Just come with me."

Mystified and mortified, Kelly stood. She let the man lead her.

*

On her bed, Kelly opened her eyes. She stared around in amazement. Everything was the way it had been earlier. Her door was shut, the curtain was closed. She was alone.

Taking several deep breaths, Kelly's mind whirled. *"What the hell had just happened? Had she really even left the room?"*

Kelly shook her head. It had to have been a nightmare. She knew something horrendous was happening. This place, this institute, was not a helpful place.

"What were they doing to her? How was she going to stop whatever was happening?"

Still sitting up in the bed, Kelly pushed her head back against the pillow. She closed her eyes and shook her head. Her hands went up and covered her face. She wanted to cry, to scream, to do something. She just had no idea what she could do.

A moment later, Kelly watched her door open. Nurse Parker stepped in, carrying a food tray. Kelly frowned, thinking the nurse had just barely been in with the breakfast she hadn't eaten.

Smiling at Kelly, Susan moved over and placed the tray on the table. She swung the table, so it sat over Kelly's lap, like earlier.
"I'm glad to see you awake. I brought lunch earlier, but you were sound asleep. I didn't wake you. Your body needs its' rest. I decided to bring you dinner instead. A nice light meal, soup and a sandwich. I want you to try and eat this. Your body needs nourishment. If you don't start eating, I'm afraid the doctor will order an IV to get the nutrients your body needs. I don't know about you, but personally, I'd rather get my vitamins and minerals in food."

Staring at the woman, Kelly was trying to assess what the nurse had just said. Could it really be time for the evening meal? Had she been asleep, or was what happened to her based in some weird reality? Was her mind causing everything because of whatever trauma she had recently dealt with?
In her heart, Kelly didn't think so. It was this place, these people. Why? Kelly had no answers and no resolutions. She thought back to when the nurse had been in her room earlier.

Susan had given Kelly, what she was told, was an antibiotic. Was it something different, something that had brought on the strange dream, or whatever it was that had happened?

Kelly sighed, more confused than ever.

She looked down at the meal Nurse Parker had brought. She wondered now, if there was even something being put into her food. Then again, she hadn't touched her breakfast.

Kelly's stomach grumbled loudly.

Susan Parker smiled. "I heard that. You may not think you're hungry, but your stomach says otherwise. Go on, eat your dinner."

Staring at the food, Kelly knew the woman was right. Nodding, she slowly began eating. She tried to ignore Nurse Parker, watching her.

A short time later, Kelly had finished almost the whole meal. She pushed the few bites of sandwich, and the last of her soup, to the far side of her tray. She gave Susan a crooked smile and a nod.

"I'm stuffed. But you're right. I do feel better with a full stomach. Thanks for bringing it in."

With a grin, Susan nodded.

"Of course, that's what I am here for. Now, can I get you anything else? I have several more patients to see. Doctor Anders should be coming to see you any minute. I know he is on this unit doing rounds."

Kelly shook her head.
"No, unless you found me something to read."

Nurse Parker shrugged and reached for Kelly's tray. "Sorry, I haven't found time to do that yet. I better get that cleared with one of the doctors as well. I wouldn't want to do the wrong thing. If I see Doctor Anders, I'll check and make sure you can handle that."

Kelly frowned, wondering what kind of hospital didn't let the patients watch television, or even have some kind of reading material. Right now, she didn't want to argue. So she only nodded and then watched Susan Parker leave the room.
The sound of the door shutting, reminded Kelly that the thing would be locked. She wanted to get out of bed, run to the door, and pound on it. Knowing it would be one of the nurses or the doctors, who she didn't think she could trust, coming to answer her pleas, Kelly knew she wouldn't resort to that tactic.

She laid back against her pillow and waited to see who would be coming to the door next. Susan had said Doctor Anders. Kelly wondered if the man would be as strange as Doctor Mengle.

She didn't have to wait long. Fifteen minutes after the nurse left, the door opened. Kelly stared at the person who entered. The man, also wearing a white coat, like Doctor Mengle, was closer to what Kelly thought her age was. She had no way to know for certain, but the image she'd seen in the mirror had her guessing she was in her thirties. The blonde haired man, with dark brown eyes looked about the same age to Kelly.

He moved in the room, and closed the door behind him. The action left Kelly with the feeling that when anyone left her room, they had to hand lock the door. To Kelly, it didn't seem as if the door just locked by itself, when it was shut.

The doctor stepped closer.
"Good evening Kelly. My name is Doctor Anders. I work here at the institute with Doctor Mengle. Nurse Parker tells me you are feeling better. It's good to see you are finally eating. Now, I'd just like to ask you a couple of questions. Do you feel up to that?" He waited for Kelly to give him a nod, before he began the questioning.
"Are you having any headaches?"

Kelly shrugged, but nodded. She was almost afraid, if she said yes, more medication would be given.
"I have been having some headaches. Mostly I feel the pain begin, but it goes away fairly quickly. The pain isn't bothering me long enough to even think about."

The doctor nodded. Unlike Doctor Mengle, Doctor Anders didn't carry a clipboard or a pen. Kelly was happy for that. The sound of Doctor Mengle's clicking pen, was enough to trigger a headache.

"What about strange flashes of light?"

Thinking of what she had just went through, Kelly felt her nerves tighten. Nurse Parker had said Kelly had been asleep for most of the day. The strange incident Kelly had suffered through, didn't feel like a dream and the strange lights had prevented her from seeing what was going on around her. She nodded. "Yes, I'd say I've had strange lights interrupting my normal vision. Does that mean something is wrong? Is that a result of the accident?"

Giving Kelly a small smile, the doctor shook his head.
"No, nothing is wrong. After a head injury, all sorts of problems are found. Most go away in a week or two. Right now, I'd say there isn't anything to worry about. How about strange dreams? Are you suffering from those?"

Staring at the doctor, Kelly had a feeling she should keep the episode she had just gone through, to herself. She wasn't sure why, but for now, she felt silence was the best avenue to take.
She shook her head.
"I don't think my dreams are anything out of the normal range of dreams. They are funny things though, aren't they?"

The doctor nodded, knowing Kelly was lying.

"Yes, the mind uses our dream state in unusual ways. From what you told me, I think your recovery is coming along well."

Kelly shrugged. "I am a bit bored just sitting in this room. I was told I can't watch television. I don't have a radio, a phone, or anything like that. I would love to have a book or a magazine to read, just to pass the time."

Phil Anders nodded.
"I think we could find you a magazine or two to read. We have found that too much stimulus, soon after an accident, delays recovery. After all, our first concern here is to get you feeling better."

Kelly sighed. "Then maybe I can go home."
In her mind she was thinking, *wherever that is*.
She was afraid to say those words though.

The doctor however, used Kelly's comment to ask one more question. The same one she was thinking of. He was frowning as he spoke.
"Have you remembered where your home is?"

A sigh escaped Kelly's lips. She felt like breaking down and crying, but forced herself to keep steady. "No, but I have been getting a few pictures in my head about my past. They fly by so quickly, but I am hoping one of these times, everything will come through and my memory will return."

Phil nodded, although he knew that wasn't going to
happen. Most people who ended up at the institute,
stayed there.
He gave Kelly an encouraging look. His dark brown
eyes appearing lighter with the motion.
"You never know what miracles are waiting to
happen. I need to get going now. You just rest and
I'll see what I can do about that reading material."

Kelly smiled with relief.
"Thanks so much, Doctor Anders, I think that would
help me alot."

The Doctor turned and walked to the door and let
himself out of the room.
When the door closed, Kelly tried to decide what she
thought of the man. Doctor Anders seemed kinder
than Doctor Mengle. Something about the man felt
familiar to her as well. Kelly didn't know how that
was possible, but it was on top of her mind, no
matter if the reasoning was true, or just a false
memory her brain was conjuring up.

It was Nurse Adams, who entered Kelly's room next.
Like her feelings distinguishing Doctor Mengle,
from Doctor Anders, Kelly also had differing
feelings about the two nurses she had met.
Susan Parker seemed friendlier than Barbara Adams.
There was something about the woman, standing in
her room at the moment, that bothered Kelly.
Barbara Adams attitude towards her seemed a bit
harsh. Kelly wondered how bad that attitude would

be if Nurse Adams knew about her snooping around earlier. Kelly hadn't had a lot of time to think about what she had found in the closet. She also knew, that was something, she wouldn't share with anyone she had met so far at the institute.

Nurse Adams again had her hair pulled back away from her face. Kelly thought the ponytail was so tight it must be pulling the rust colored hair out by the roots. She stared at Kelly.

"I just talked to Nurse Parker as we prepared to switch shifts. She tells me you not only ate your dinner, but were able to have a long nap this afternoon. That's a good thing. You probably feeling like you are sleeping too much, but with a head injury, after we make sure you don't have long term damage, we like you to get plenty of rest. In fact I've come in tonight to bring you your muscle relaxer. It is the same medication you had last night."

Kelly could see the stern look on nurse Adams' face. She wanted to say no, but felt that would cause problems. Kelly wondered if she could pretend to take the pill and spit it out later.

She nodded at Barbara.

"Yes, both of the doctors I have seen, think the best thing for me to do is rest. I guess I was worried that too much sleep would make me worse."

Barbara shook her head.

"Well, the doctors went to school for a lot of years to even be considered to work at this institute. You're lucky to have them taking care of you. The best thing you can do is follow their orders."

Hearing Barbara say the word 'orders' made Kelly anxious. It was like she was in a jail and not a hospital. Kelly took the pill the nurse held out. Grabbing the cup of water on the table near her bed, she slipped the pill in her mouth and took a drink. Instead of trying to hide the pill somewhere in her mouth, Kelly swallowed the thing. She was angry at herself for doing that. She'd have to try again next time she got a pill. Kelly was sure she would be getting the. so called, antibiotic. in the daytime and another muscle relaxer at night.
She could see Nurse Adams was preparing to leave and she frowned.
"Has there been any news on who my family is? I'm sure they must be worried about me."

Barbara shook her head. Her lips straightened in a grim line. Kelly wasn't sure if that was because there had been no news, or because Barbara was mad at her for even asking.
"No, we've been checking the name you gave us with the authorities around the area, but no one has heard anything about a Kelly Mitchell being missing. I'm sorry."

Watching the nurse, Kelly was certain the woman wasn't sorry at all. She sighed as Nurse Adams walked to the door.

As she opened it, she grinned at Kelly.
"Sweet dreams."

The two words, said in a smirking voice, instead of
being comforting, sent chills down Kelly's spine.
She stared at the closed door in horror and disbelief.

Chapter 5

Kelly sat on the bed, her mind reeling.
She hadn't liked the way Nurse Adams had spoken
her departing words. Kelly wondered if her head
injury was twisting her judgement. Maybe the nurse
hadn't sounded the way Kelly had thought.
Kelly sighed, knowing her first thought was
probably the right one.
There was something strange about Nurse Adams.
Something dark.
Kelly covered her mouth as she yawned. She wished
she had been able to stop herself from swallowing
that damn pill. The doctors and nurses said she
needed sleep, but Kelly thought, if her body need
sleep, or anything else, it would automatically take
care of the craving. She didn't need pills to help with
that. She tried to keep her eyes open, but they were
drooping down, no matter how hard she fought the
inevitable, and dreaded the sleep, that she knew, was
coming.

The dream felt real. Kelly was still in a bed, or
something similar to one. Whatever she was laying
on, wasn't as soft as the bed in her room.
The room itself was bright. Looking above her,
Kelly could see a glowing light, straight above her
head. She could hear the sound of crying.
Turning her head to the right, she saw, what looked
somewhat like, nothing more than a cot, but she
knew it was an operating table. That thought made
her realize, she also was on a similar table.

The young woman next to her, looked much younger than Kelly did. Kelly could see the woman grabbing her long blonde hair in her hands. Along with the crying, the sounds of moans could be heard.
Kelly could almost feel the woman's pain.

The young woman yelled.
"Make it stop. Please, I can't take it. Stop it, please, stop it."

Hearing another noise, Kelly turned away from the woman. She watched Doctor Mengle step into the room.
He went straight over to stand by the other woman. "Gina, you know better. Stop that yelling. You have work to do. You need to stop acting like this. You'll scare Kelly. You wouldn't want to do that would you?"

Turning her head, Gina stared at Kelly with baby blue eyes. She looked scared to death. Her head turned from side to side. Her voice trembled and broke up with her crying.
"Of course not. Kelly knows I wouldn't do that. She knows we stick together and watch out for each other."

Staring at the girl, Kelly wanted to say that she knew nothing like that. She didn't even know this woman the doctor had called Gina. Then again, Kelly also was thinking, she did know Gina. Somehow, somewhere, the two did know each other.

Kelly didn't speak, waiting to see what the doctor would say. Him, she knew, for sure.

It was only a moment later, Doctor Mengle nodded and spoke. His voice less harsh than it had been. "Good, I'm glad to hear that. Now, if your hysterics are over, we can get on with the experiment."
Leaving Gina's side, the doctor moved over to Kelly. Reaching over on a table he grabbed what looked like a wire that was almost as thick as a pencil. He smiled at Kelly. To Kelly, the smile looked like something a shark might look like if it smiled.
"I'm going to attach this to the back of your neck. Don't worry it won't hurt. This will help us read the results better. Just stay still."
Reaching under Kelly's neck, the doctor attached the wire. She could feel that his hand was cold and clammy. She tried to stop the shiver that ran through her. The doctor didn't seem to notice. He stood back.
"See, that didn't hurt at all. Now, both of you just need to lie still. I will be in the next room. Just remember, I can see both of you from there. Don't try anything, either of you will regret."

Kelly couldn't imagine what either her, or Gina, could try. The doctor was in charge and calling all the shots.
He turned and left the room, as Kelly was making that observation inside her head. She didn't dare say anything like that aloud.

A moment later, Kelly felt a tingling at the back of her neck. The sensation intensified until it felt like she was being stung by a bee every few seconds. It hurt, but she didn't dare yell out. Turning her head toward Gina, Kelly could see pain etched on the younger woman's face.

The sound of the doctor's voice could be heard in the room. Kelly thought there must be some kind of speaker set up.

"I need both of you to concentrate. There is a baseball on the counter. Imagine it in your mind. You don't need to look at it. Just think of that ball. Close your eyes. Picture the baseball. As soon as you can see it in your mind, I want both of you to imagine picking it up and throwing it. You can do this. Now, see the ball, pick it up, and throw it."

Closing her eyes, Kelly tried to do as she was told. Her mind couldn't focus. Suddenly she felt a shock to the back of her neck. As she screamed out, she heard the woman next to her do the same.
Then she yelled.
"Stop it. We're trying."

The doctor's voice could be heard, after a maniacal laugh had sounded.
"Do as your told, or the next shock will be much stronger."

Squeezing her eyes tighter, Kelly concentrated.

A moment later, she opened her eyes and realized Gina must have done the same. Kelly watched in amazement as a baseball flew across the room and smashed into the wall.

The doctor's voice sounded ecstatic when he spoke. "Well done, well done. I knew you two could do this. Now, we need to try something a bit harder. In the corner of the room, there is a metal basket. It is filled with paper and wood chips. Both of you, concentrate on that basket. Think of it on fire. Push with your minds. Light the paper and chips on fire. Do it now."

Eyes closed, Kelly concentrated. She didn't actually know what the metal basket looked like, but she held an image in her mind anyway. She could see the paper as it turned a brownish color with the heat. Then, a moment later, she could smell something burning, see fire burning in the basket.

Kelly's eyes opened as she heard the sound of the doctor running in the room. He carried a fire extinguisher. He sprayed the metal basket, putting out the flames. He stared at the area at moment, Kelly was sure she heard him whispering under his breath. To her, it sounded like he said.
"A new weapon."

Placing the extinguisher on the floor, the doctor turned to look at the two women. His eyes were shining brightly.

"Well done, well done. I think that will be enough for tonight's session."

He stepped over to Gina. Reaching behind her head, the doctor removed the wire.

Moving over to Kelly, he repeated the procedure. The doctor walked over and stood between the two women, close to their feet, and smiled.

"The two of you work very well together. Next time, I think we will try something bigger. For now, you did well."

Gina's light blue eyes turned dark with anger. "There won't be a next time. What the hell is wrong with you? How can you call yourself a doctor? How can you treat people like this? Every time you do this, I have headaches for days. You are killing us. I know you are. I can feel it."

The doctor laughed. "Now Gina, you're exaggerating. I'm not killing either of you. In fact, I am making you better. What the two of you will be able to accomplish, when my experiments are completed, will astound the world. You will be almost as famous as I."

Leaning over, Gina spit on the floor. "That's what I think about you, and your experiments. You're crazy, damn it. What kind of monster are you?"

Watching the exchange, Kelly was astounded by Gina's bravery, she also knew the woman shouldn't have said the things she had. Kelly could see the anger in Doctor Mengle's eyes. A moment later, the look was wiped off his face.

Kelly knew the anger was still there though, and she worried for Gina. She didn't know what Doctor Mengle was capable of, but she was sure it was something horrendous. She wanted to yell at Gina. To tell her to be quiet. To warn her of the danger, but as she opened her mouth to speak, Kelly woke up from the strange dream.

*

She couldn't get her breath. Kelly gulped for air. She looked around, realizing she was in the room where she had first fallen asleep. She wasn't on an operating table, but in a hospital bed.

She looked around, expecting to see Gina in the room with her. Instead, she realized she was alone. That thought depressed her.

The dream, or rather the nightmare, had been so real. Not seeing Gina by her side, even if it had been a dream, was like losing her best friend.

Reaching up, Kelly covered her face with her hands and began crying.

What was happening? Who was Gina? Why did she feel like, somehow, the two of them really did know each other?

Was she just having a super, realistic dream, or was something more happening? Something so strange, it felt impossible.

Oh my hell, what was really going on in the strange place everyone called Pine View Institute?

Shaking her head, Kelly closed her eyes and, although it was the last thing she wanted to do, fell back asleep.

Chapter 6

Kelly only woke, when the sound of the door opening, jarred her from a now, thankfully, dreamless sleep.
She stared in horror as the man from her nightmare stepped into the room.

Carrying his clipboard, Doctor Mengle pulled a chair over toward Kelly's bed.
"How are we feeling today?"

Not sure how to answer the question, Kelly shrugged.

"I'm doing alright I guess."

The doctor frowned.
"Are you still having headaches?"

A shrug was followed by a nod.
"They come and go."

Nodding, the doctor stared at Kelly.
"Are you seeing unusual colors or having strange dreams?"

Kelly sighed, wondering where the questioning was leading. She also wondered if she should tell this man, who she couldn't force herself to trust, the truth. Finally she decided to answer with what was probably what someone might call a half-truth. One

thing she didn't want to share was Mengle's
appearance in her nightmares.

"Yes, I am having a few problems with both those
things."

The doctor nodded, his pen clicking. The sound was
bringing on a headache that Kelly didn't need.
"I thought that was the case. I'm ordering a CT scan
of your head. I'm afraid you have have suffered
more damage than I was aware of."
The doctor stood.
"Someone should be in soon to escort you to the
radiology lab. Just rest until they get here. I'll tell
Nurse Adams to hold off on your breakfast until after
the testing is complete. I'll also ask her to draw some
blood when she makes her visit."

Without waiting for a response from Kelly, the
doctor turned and hurried out of the room.

After the door shut behind the man, Kelly let out a
breath of relief. She frowned, thinking about just
how real her nightmare actually was. Her hand
slipped behind her neck, feeling for a sore spot or a
scab to prove her dream had been real. The lines on
her forehead deepened. She did feel a sore spot.
Getting out of bed, Kelly headed into the bathroom.
She twisted her head as she looked in the mirror. She
couldn't quite turn to the right position to see the
back of her neck, but she could see the area was
reddish colored. She gasped, as she thought about
what her finding could mean. She had worried the

pills she was being given, were not what she was being told they were. Something horrendous was happening at the Pine View Institute. Something she knew she had no way to escape. Kelly forced away the tears that threatened. The last thing she needed was to fall to pieces. Doing that would seal her fate. Heading back to her bed, Kelly needed to think. Somehow, she needed to find a way out of this crazy place. Being inside the walls of the institute was more like being in a lunatic asylum, than not. Before Kelly was able to even begin to think abut finding a solution to her problem, the door to her room opened.

A young man, pushing an empty wheelchair, stepped into the room.
"Hi, I'm Scott, Doctor Mengle has asked for me to take you to the radiology lab. I'm sure you can walk just fine, but rules are rules. I need to take you to the lab in this wheelchair. We wouldn't want to take a chance of you falling and getting hurt."

Kelly frowned, but slid her legs off the bed. She tried to grin at the man, who she thought must be an intern or something similar.
"I can understand that. I mean I'm sure for insurance purposes you wouldn't want a patient to get hurt." She moved over and sat in the chair. Despite her statement, Kelly was thinking that the institute was actually causing harm.

As she was pushed from her room to the radiology lab, Kelly tried to focus her attention on anything and everything. She mostly was watching for a doorway that might lead to the outside. The trip was short and Kelly didn't see anything that seemed even remotely connected to the outside world. The hallways she was pushed in, didn't even have windows. In the radiology lab, Kelly was moved from the wheelchair to a table. The young man helped her get situated in a supine position before he headed out of the room.

A technician came in the room and spoke to Kelly. "Looks like we'll be getting some pictures of your head today. You're lucky, the CT scan is much shorter than an MRI. I will need you to stay still." The man pointed at the machine, positioned at the end of Kelly's position.
"This machine will run over your head and back several times. You will hear a voice telling you to hold your breath several times. Just follow any instructions you hear and this will be over in no time."

Kelly nodded she understood, but didn't talk. As the machine took its' pictures, Kelly had time to think. Mostly her thoughts were on the woman who had been in the nightmare with her. Kelly still hadn't decided if the events she had experienced were happening real time, or if what she had was a dream recalling the atrocities she had endured at a different time. No matter which, Kelly had come to the conclusion the whole thing was based in some kind of reality. She wondered and worried about the woman who the doctor had called Gina. Was she locked in a room as well? Did she have memories of her past? Something Kelly was finding elusive. The only real recollection had come when she had first seen the shoes in the bottom of the closet in her room. Kelly decided when she got back to her room, and when no nurses or doctors were around, she needed to have another look in that closet. She hoped taking another hard look at the shoes would trigger more events from her past. The wanderings of her mind stopped when the technician stepped in the room.

"We're done with the scan. You did a great job. I'll get the results up to Doctor Mengle. I'm sure he'll be sharing the findings with you."

Hearing the statement, Kelly was just as sure, that the doctor may tell her something, but it wouldn't be the truth.

The man who had brought Kelly to the room, came back in, pushing the wheelchair.
"Time to get you back to your room."

Wishing for a tour of the facility and knowing better than to ask, Kelly was instead taken straight back to what she had begun to think of as a jail cell, instead of a hospital room.
Getting on her bed, she watched the man leave.
Kelly decided the closet examination better wait. She

expected a nurse to come check on her soon. She didn't know the time, but figured it was well past breakfast.

Her thoughts were confirmed when Nurse Adams stepped in the room. Her reddish hair was still pulled back severely from her face. Only today it was in a braid. She carried the food tray she held to the table, next to Kelly's bed. She also held what looked like a plastic basket.

"I'm sorry you missed breakfast. I hear you were having a CT Scan. I arranged to get your lunch tray just a bit early."

After moving the table to slide over Kelly's lap, the nurse held up the basket type holder.

"Doctor Mengle has asked me to get some blood samples from you. If I do that now, will it interrupt your meal?"

Kelly shook her head and straightened her arm.

"Go ahead and take the samples. I'll eat when you're done."

Nodding, Nurse Adams went about her business. Taking the samples didn't take long. When she had them, the nurse stared at Kelly.

"If you don't need anything else, I need to get these down to the lab for testing. Doctor Mengle is anxious for the results."

Kelly shrugged. "I'm fine. I'll just go ahead and have my meal now."

Actually, Kelly was glad the woman wasn't sticking around. She liked Nurse Parker better than the woman in her room this morning, but she really didn't trust either of them.

Once alone, Kelly had only a few bites of her food before pushing the tray aside. She wondered if the food, or drinks, she was receiving, might be drugged. She had no idea what type of drugs enhanced strange supernatural powers, but felt the doctors and nurses must be aware of some. How else could she and Gina throw a ball with their minds or start a fire? She felt in her heart, that had actually happened.
Kelly sighed, knowing she had plenty of time for contemplation of the strange phenomenons.
Right now, she wanted to get another look in the closet.

Leaving her bed, Kelly headed for the closet.
Before she opened the door, she instead decided to peek out the window. Pulling back the curtain, Kelly stared out. She was disappointed to see nothing had changed from the last time she had looked out. She thought it might be summertime. Although most of the trees sitting outside the window were evergreens, Kelly saw a few other varieties. Because the leaves on those was also of a green colored variation, she was sure fall hadn't yet arrived. Because the leaves were full, she had a feeling spring had passed.
With a sigh, Kelly let the curtain drop closed.
She turned to the closet. Opening the door, she stared at the shoes a minute before bending down and

picking them up. She carried the shoes with her, holding them close, like they were a treasure of sorts. She made her way to the chair Doctor Mengle had so recently vacated.

Sitting down, Kelly looked at her feet, clad in hospital socks. Although not much thicker than average socks, the material on the bottom had non-skid tread. Kelly hoped they wouldn't interfere with the fit of the shoes.

Slipping on the shoes, Kelly smiled. She had been almost positive they belonged to her. The way the shoes fit, endorsed her assumption.

Sitting back, Kelly closed her eyes. Before she had a moment to think about it, the flashback began.

She was running, or more like jogging. After a block, Kelly slowed to a fast walk, then jogged again as she hit the next block. It was in the period of walking, that she heard the sound of a car, pulling over next to her.

A man, on the passenger side, leaned out the open window. In the flashback, Kelly couldn't hear anything. She could see the man waving a map and figured he and the driver were lost.

Opening the door, the man stepped out of the car. Kelly could see herself grin and nod. She knew she was offering to help. As the man stepped closer, he started raising his arm. With another step, he was at Kelly's side. The arm went around her head and the man covered her mouth with his hand. Kelly saw herself squirming, trying to fight. A moment later, she realized her attempts had been to no avail. She was being dragged by the man and thrown into the backseat of the vehicle.

Kelly frowned, not seeing her body sitting up. She wondered if the man had used something to knock her out. Kelly's heart dropped as the car sped away and the flashback vanished.

Light brown eyes flew open. Kelly felt her heart pounding in her chest. Both hands flew up covering the area in an attempt to slow the rapid beat.

Kelly stared in horror, as the door to her room began to open. Knowing she couldn't let anyone see her in such a state of anguish, Kelly stood and ran to the bathroom, pulling the door shut behind her.

A knock sounded on the door just seconds after Kelly had pulled it closed. She drew in a deep breath. The sound of Nurse Adams' voice could be heard. "Are you okay Kelly?"

Moving over toward the toilet, Kelly answered back. "I'm fine, I'll be right out."

Closing the toilet lid, Kelly sat down and covered her face with her hands. She knew she had to get her emotions under control before she let anyone see her. Removing her hands, Kelly took several slow breaths. Feeling better, she flushed the toilet, she hadn't used. Hoping outside the door, Nurse Adams would be convinced that she had just been using the facilities. Going to the sink, Kelly turned on the water. Running her hands under the cool liquid,

Kelly leaned down and splashed her face. Grabbing the towel near the sink, Kelly dried her hands and face. Looking in the mirror, Kelly saw she still looked upset, but felt she would pass inspection, once she stepped from the room.
Opening the door, Kelly moved out of the bathroom. Seeing Nurse Adams staring at her, Kelly forced a grin .

The motion wasn't reciprocated. Instead Barbara frowned and pointed at Kelly's food tray.
"You hardly touched your food."

Kelly shrugged. "Guess I wasn't very hungry."
Moving past the nurse, Kelly headed for the bed. As she sat on the edge, she realized she still had on the shoes she had found in the closet. Looking at Nurse Adams, Kelly realized Barbara had also noticed.
She pointed at Kelly's feet.
"Where did you get those?"

Staring back, Kelly frowned.
"They were in the closet. I actually was looking for something to wear. I feel funny wearing these pajamas day and night. I tried on the shoes to see if they would fit. I thought they must be mine since they were in the closet. Do I also have clothes around here some place?"

Barbara shook her head.
"When you were brought here, the clothes you had on were beyond saving. That's why you were given

the pajamas to wear. The shoes were cleaned up, and worth saving. That's why they were put in the closet. I really see no need for you to wear them though. Right now, you aren't doing anything, or going anywhere, that requires you to have shoes on."

Kelly shrugged.
"I feel better with them on. I can't say why."

Barbara shrugged. "You can leave them on I guess. If I was you, I'd slip them off before you get up on your bed, though. You may not have noticed but we haven't had a cleaning crew for a week. You just can't get good help anymore."
Barbara sighed. "Well never mind that. Right now, it's time for your antibiotic."

Kelly frowned. "Is that really necessary? Yesterday when I took one, I was so tired."

Shaking her head, Barbara reached in her pocket and pulled out a bottle of pills, Shaking one out, she handed it to Kelly.
"The doctor knows what you need. He is the one with several degrees, after all. I'd say you have enough problems without adding an infection to it."

Taking the pill, Kelly slipped it in her mouth. Using her tongue, she pushed the pill to the top of her mouth between her cheek and her teeth, hoping Nurse Adams didn't notice.
Barbara pushed a cup of water toward Kelly.

"Better have a drink to wash that down."

Lifting the cup, Kelly took a drink. She swallowed the water, careful to not let the pill slip from it's hiding spot. She could taste the bitterness of the pill as it tried to dissolve in her mouth. Kelly tried not to grimace. She noticed Nurse Adams staring at her face. When Kelly placed the cup back on the table, Nurse Adams nodded.
"There now, that wasn't so bad. Nurse Parker will be bringing your dinner tonight. I have to leave a little bit early. She will also bring your muscle relaxer tonight. I don't want to hear you gave her any problems or arguments about taking that medication either."
Brown eyes narrowed, as Nurse Adams picked up the lunch tray.
"I'll just leave you to get some rest. I do have other patients to get to."

Kelly frowned. "Has anyone found out anything about my family? I'm sure they must be worried sick."

Barbara shook her head. The red hair, pulled back so tightly, didn't move with the motion.
"No one has heard anything yet. I'm sure Doctor Mengle must have talked to the police to see if there have been reports of missing persons that fit your description."

Hearing the nurse's statement, Kelly got the feeling that Doctor Mengle hadn't bothering doing anything like that. Nurse Adams hadn't actually stated the doctor had reached the police. She had just said, more or less, that he might have done it. Kelly didn't question the statement, knowing nothing she said would matter. Instead she asked a different question. "Did you find me something to read?"

Nurse Adams shook her head.
"I've been quite busy. I'll try to mention that to Nurse Parker before I go off shift. Maybe she can dig up a magazine or two for you to look at."

Watching Nurse Adams leave the room, Kelly sighed. Having something to read, was the least of her problems. When the door had closed, Kelly waited a few minutes before she spit out the partially dissolved pill. Standing up she hurried into the bathroom and flushed the pill down the toilet. After making sure the pill had gone down, Kelly headed to the sink and rinsed the bitter taste from her mouth. Grabbing the toothbrush and toothpaste she had been given, Kelly also brushed her teeth. Glad when she finished the bitterness was gone, Kelly went back out into her room. She smiled, thinking her first attempt at not taking any more pills had at least partially worked. She didn't think much of the medicine had been ingested, She hoped later she would have as good of luck with her other medication. If she could avoid ever having to take the medication the institute put out, Kelly felt that was a good thing.

Taking off her shoes, Kelly got up on the bed. She didn't put the head down. Preferring to sit up to avoid any possibility of falling asleep, and having strange nightmares, that she was afraid, were actually reality.

Kelly knew she needed a plan to get out of this institute, but had no idea how to even begin.

Chapter 7

Sitting in the chair in her room, a deep frown sliced across Kelly's forehead. It had been three days since she'd swallowed any pills. She was positive now, the medications she'd been given before, were not what she was told they were. All she had to do was look around to know the truth. When she had first awoken in her bed, she had thought this place was a hospital. She knew the doctors and nurses called it an institute. Kelly was sure now that the word the others used, was much more accurate.
She had been under the impression this place was a newer facility. That had all began to change as Kelly pulled medications from her mouth and threw them in the toilet to be flushed away.
She was actually surprised she had gotten away with doing that for the last three days.
In fact, Nurse Adams had just left the room after bringing Kelly's lunch, and the pill, Kelly had been told was an antibiotic.
Over the last few days, Kelly had gotten better at pretending to take the medicine, and then spitting it out, and flushing it down the toilet, once she was alone.
The good news was, with her awake most of the time, neither of the institutes doctors had taken her from her room. The bad news was, that also meant she hadn't been taken to a room where the woman she knew only as Gina was. Kelly had been visited by the doctors, but when they saw she was awake, they hadn't stayed in her room long.

That scared her.
What were they really doing the times she had been
transferred from her room to various lab settings?
She had to figure the same thing was being done to
others being held hostage in the dingy walls of the
institute.

For Kelly, the biggest change and concern, was the
appearance of her room, now that the drugs were out
of her system.
The white walls looked a dingy color. The curtain
that covered the window, that couldn't open, was
torn and stained. She glanced outside at least once a
day, hoping to see someone outside. Although she
hadn't decided what to do if she did. Banging the
window and screaming, she might only get in more
trouble. What if the person outside was in cahoots
with the doctors and nurses in this insane institute?
What miseries would they dump on her then?
Kelly had also noticed a few small cracks in the
walls, and ceiling of her room. She had come to the
realization that more than just drugs had to have
been used on her. She thought of hypnosis, and
wondered if the use of such a thing, could alter
reality. She felt like she was going crazy. Was the
world around her what she had seen before, or what
she was actually experiencing now?

Kelly was able to shower. But when the pills wore
off, her showers got shorter. The shower stall was as
run-down as the rest of the things in her shrunken
world.

Overwhelmed by her thoughts, Kelly dropped her head in her hands, and allowed herself to cry.

It took ten minutes, or longer, before Kelly was able to wipe away the tears. She needed to try and focus her mind on something more than self pity.

She had to make a plan to escape this institute of horrors.

Because no one had taken her from the room in the last few days, she had no connection with the young woman she had been with in the lab. Kelly knew the woman's name was Gina, but not much else. She had so many questions and not many answers.

Kelly grunted at that thought. The truth was, she had no answers.

She had finally been given a couple of magazines to look at. One look at the tattered covers and Kelly knew the publications were out of date. Still, even reading old articles, and stories, inside the faded covers helped pass the time. She had also noticed, that despite her problems with her memory of her life, she could easily remember the things she saw in the magazines. One of the magazines was a publication featuring celebrities. Kelly easily recognized the people in the photos, from television and movies, she had watched. Why could she remember people she had only seen in the media and not her own family? Kelly wondered if her being given outdated magazines was done on purpose. It seemed those at the institute went out of their way to

confuse her. She had no television, no radio, no phone, no calendar, and no clock in her room.
The passage of time was mostly only noted by the difference in the three meals she was brought each day. She could go to the window and try to estimate the time of day or night, but had no accurate way to measure time.

One difference was on what had to be weekend days. On those two days, different nurses came to her room. A man and a woman covered the shifts when Kelly guessed Nurse Adams and Nurse Parker must have days off. Neither of the two seemed to be any kinder than the other nurses, and Kelly was sure they weren't in the category of allies.

In the chair, Kelly tried to think. There had to be a way out. Not just for her, but for Gina, and any others, who were trapped in this horrendous place, where reality was distorted.

Chapter 8

While Kelly was racking her brain for a solution, Doctor Mengle was seated in his office. He had stopped Nurse Adams, during her rounds, and asked for both her, and Nurse Parker, to come to his office when they prepared for their shift change. The one time the two were together at the institute.

Now, the two women sat in uncomfortable chairs staring at the doctor. Both were nervous. The doctor seldom asked to meet with them.
The sound of the doctor's pen clicking, was the only noise in the room, until he cleared his throat, and began speaking. His blue eyes, darkened with anger.
"Miss Mitchell is not sleeping. Why haven't the two of you been giving her the medications you were asked to?"

Both women shook there heads in dispute of the doctor's claim. Barbara was the one to speak.
"I don't know what you're talking about. I made it a point to watch Kelly take her medication."

Susan nodded. "So did I. Kelly receives her medication from me, right before she goes to bed at night."

Staring at the doctor, Barbara also nodded.
"Yes, and I have been giving her the meds in the daytime. I do my job Doctor Mengle, and don't like your accusations."

Seeing the look on the doctor's face, Barbara wondered if she had been out of line speaking to the doctor, the way she was. Mengle had the last word of everything. Barbara needed the job with its' high pay. She also knew Mengle needed to keep people who knew how to keep their mouth shut. That was one thing she had in her favor. She knew how to keep the institute's dirty secrets.

Glaring at the two women, the doctor grunted.
"I don't give a damn what either of you like or don't like. The fact is, Miss Mitchell hasn't been on those medications. I can't possibly do my job if she isn't taking the pills. I asked the two of you to give her those meds. I expect my orders to be followed."
Opening a drawer in his desk, the doctor pulled out a vile of clear liquid.
"From now on, the two of you will be giving Miss Mitchell her medication with a shot. This will ensure the medication gets into her system."

A frown appeared on Barbara's face.
Her brown eyes narrowed.
"What is that?"

The doctor shrugged and shook his head.
"All either of you need to know, and all Miss Mitchell needs to be told, is this is a vitamin B-12 shot. I know she was complaining about her energy level. Just explain to her that vitamin B-12 shots help with that. It doesn't matter what the subject asks or objects to anyway. We aren't here to please the

patients. The experiments must continue. Both of you know how important my work is."

Both nurses stared at Doctor Mengle. The two weren't privy to what the experiments entailed. They had only been told that the, government sponsored institute, was doing important work of national security. They didn't question the doctors' motives. Not just the man in the room with them, but also the work being done by Doctor Anders.

The two nurses nodded their understanding. Both knew they were lucky to just get reprimanded, and not fired, for not insuring Kelly Mitchell was actually taking the medication they had given her.

Doctor Mengle handed the vial to Nurse Parker.
"I want Miss Mitchell to get her first shot this evening."
He turned to look at Nurse Adams.
"You will administer a dose in the afternoon as well, right after lunch."

Barbara's eyes narrowed. "What about Kelly's other medication. Should I continue giving her that, and making sure she swallows the damn pills?"

The Doctor shook his head.
"No, the shots will be sufficient. I want to warn both of you. If Miss Mitchell isn't asleep, and soundly, the next time I enter her room, your jobs are on the line."

The doctors' gaze dropped to look at some papers on his desk. A moment later he looked up at the nurses and grunted before speaking.

"The two of you are dismissed. Get the hell out of my office."

Knowing better than to give a retort, the two women stood and quickly left the room. Once they walked into the hallway, Barbara turned to Susan and spoke in a quiet voice.

"Oh hell, I had no inkling that Kelly wasn't taken the pills we gave her. She didn't act any differently that I could see."

Susan shrugged. "I don't spend enough time with her to judge. That will change tonight. Her dinner will be late since, Mister high and mighty in there, needed to complain about the job we are doing. After she eats, I'll give her the shot."

Susan frowned as she stared at Barbara.

"What do you really think is in this vial?"

Rolling her eyes, Barbara shook her head.

"To tell you the truth, I don't want to know. I admire Doctor Mengle and Doctor Adams for the work they do and the results they get. I think the intricate details of how they both get things accomplished is something better left unknown. I'm happy to receive my paycheck, with no questions asked."

A nod came from Susan, although she wasn't as adamant about the doctors methods, as her fellow worker. For Susan, the excellent pay, and benefits, kept her on the job. Although she didn't like some of the things she saw inside the walls of the institute, she knew to keep her mouth shut.
"I better get started on my rounds. Have a good night Barbara."

Nodding, Barbara gave Susan a quick smile.
"I'd tell you the same, but know that would just be wishful thinking. See you in the morning."

Once Barbara left, Susan went to the nurses' office to get her things together for the night shift.

An hour later, Susan stepped in Kelly's room carrying a tray with the woman's late dinner. She gave Kelly a smile, although what she really wanted to do was scream at her patient. Susan just felt lucky that Kelly's actions hadn't gotten her fired.
"An emergency came up. Your dinner is a bit late. I'll be back shortly to pick it up."

Sitting on her bed, Kelly didn't like the anger she could see in Nurse Parker's light blue eyes. She didn't question the look, but only nodded.
"I hope everything is okay."

Susan only shrugged, then turned and left the room.

After the nurse had gone, Kelly picked at her food. Her appetite was always poor, but after seeing the look she had gotten from Nurse Parker, it was non-existent. Kelly pushed away the tray and tried to think. The only thing that came to mind was somehow the nurses had discovered that she hadn't actually been taking her pills. If that was true, Kelly knew there would be a price to pay.

A short time later, when Nurse Parker returned, Kelly found her fears had been justified.
Nurse Parker had moved the table, with the food tray, away from the bed. She held a shot needle.
"I have good news, and some not so good. I know you hate taking medication. The pills you usually get are being stopped. Doctor Mengle has asked for you to receive vitamin B-12 shots. Some of your blood tests came back and showed your levels are low. Those will have to be delivered with a shot. I'll be giving you one at night, and Nurse Adams will bring one in the daytime. I think you'll be glad for the new medication. Vitamin B-12 shots are great for giving you energy."
Even as she spoke, Susan knew what she was saying was a lie. It didn't really matter. The doctor had given the orders. Susan needed her job and if she wanted to keep it, she had to carry out orders, like them or not.

Watching Nurse Parker's face as she spoke, Kelly also knew the woman was lying. She was certain they had discovered she had been spitting out her

previous medicine. Kelly didn't ask what her other blood tests had shown, or if the CT scan results had come back. No matter what she was told about her testing, or anything else related to the institute, she was positive would be a lie anyway.
Kelly watched as Nurse Parker administered the shot. Then she pushed her head back against the pillow, waiting to see what horrors would begin.

Picking up the tray, Nurse Parker nodded at Kelly. "I'll try to check in on you later."

Kelly nodded, then frowned.
"Do you think you could you find me something else to wear? I think I've had these same pajamas on since I got here."

Looking at Kelly, Nurse Parker had a look of disgust on her face.
"I can check. Really though, you are just sitting in the room. I don't actually think your clothes have gotten dirty from that. Our cleaning crew usually takes care of the laundry. Since they quit, and haven't been replaced, we are running behind. If I can find something for you to wear, I'll drop by later with the clothes."

Kelly mumbled a quiet thanks, feeling like the nurse was mad at her for even asking. She only hoped Nurse Parker could find pants and a shirt, instead of pajamas for her. Or maybe both. Kelly doubted that would happen.

As soon as Nurse Parker left the room, Kelly reached up and rubbed her arm where the needle had gone in. She was surprised that Nurse Parker hadn't even bothered to put a bandage over the area. Kelly could see a smear of blood at the spot she had just rubbed. Slipping her legs over the side of the bed, Kelly stood up. She wanted to get to the bathroom and wash the area.

As she began the short walk, Kelly felt the room spinning, and knew she was in trouble. She was astonished by how fast whatever had been in the shot had worked.

Instead of going to the bathroom, Kelly turned and headed back for the safety of the bed. She used the control of the bed to move the head down. She didn't think being in the sitting position, she had been earlier, would help with the dizziness that was over whelming her.

Lying down, and against her better judgement Kelly closed her eyes.

*

When the light brown eyes opened again, Kelly was sitting in a chair. She could feel a sharp pain at the back of her neck and knew instinctively that Doctor Mengle was doing another experiment.

She looked around the room and saw she was alone. There was a chair sitting just a couple of feet from her right side. She frowned, wondering if it was there so someone could join her. Looking to the left, she watched the open door to the room. She only had to wait a few moments to see Gina being brought in by Doctor Mengle.

He escorted the woman to the chair. Once she sat down, the doctor went to the counter in the room. Kelly couldn't see what he held, but guessed it was some type of shot, when the doctor stepped behind Gina, and the woman let out a small gasp.
The doctor was shaking his head. Even that motion didn't mess up the man's hair. Kelly had never seen the man with a hair out of place. He was frowning. "Now Miss Harris, that didn't hurt. You have a tendency to exaggerate."

Listening to the doctor. Kelly realized this was the first time she had heard Gina's last name. She didn't know the woman, but felt that their common bond of suffering, at the hands of the institute's personnel, made them more like family, than not.

The doctor stepped away from Gina for just a moment. When he returned he carried some typed of cable. Kelly stared at it, knowing it was similar to what had been used on her and Gina before.
The doctor ran the cable from the back of Kelly's neck to the back of Gina's, joining the two in some kind of strange connection.

Kelly had an image from the movie 'Frankenstein' flash through her mind. The idea of a mad scientist was unwanted, and horrifying.

The doctor nodded as soon as he had the two tethered together.
"Okay, I will be stepping into the other room to monitor the progress of this test. I will give orders over the speaker."
The doctor pointed at a black box that sat up in one corner of the room, close to the ceiling.

As Kelly stared where the doctor was pointing, she noticed that, like before, when she had been given drugs, the ceiling and walls of the room looked new. Somewhere in the back of her mind, she knew what she was seeing wasn't real. She knew without the medication, this room, like her own, would look old and dirty. She was amazed to think a drug could do that. Trying to push the strange thought to the back of her mind, Kelly turned to look at Gina, and smiled. Smiling back, Gina stared at Kelly. The light blue eyes opened wide, as Gina's thoughts appeared in Kelly's mind.

"I thought something bad had happened to you. I've been here alone for three nights."

Kelly sighed, but tried not to move her head. She was afraid any motion would allow Doctor Mengle to know that she and Gina could communicate telepathically.

"I wasn't swallowing the medication the nurses gave me. They must have figured it out. Tonight the nurse brought a shot instead of a pill."
Kelly frowned.
"Why do you think the doctor doesn't know we can talk to each other with our minds."

Gina's blue eyes narrowed, but she too had realized it was better not to nod or shake her head.
"I don't know, I'm just glad he hasn't figured that out. I'm sorry you got a shot, but I'm glad to have you here with me."

Kelly grinned. "It is a lot better, and easier to deal with, having company."

Both women's thoughts were interrupted by the sound of the doctor's voice, coming from the black box on the wall.
"If you look at the counter in front of you both, you will see a piece of pipe. I want the two of you to focus on the pipe. I want you to bend it."

Gina's voice sounded in Kelly's head.
"I'd like to bend that pipe around his damn neck."

Trying not to laugh, Kelly answered back.
"That's probably why Doctor Mengle is staying in the other room."
Kelly then frowned.
"How long have you been at this place Gina?"

"Three months. You must have gotten here long after me. The first time I saw you was the other day."

Thinking it was amazing to talk, without opening her mouth, Kelly answered.
"I think I've been here two weeks. How big is this place? Is it the size of a regular hospital?"

Gina grunted. "It's not the size of any hospital I ever heard of, and what goes on inside this building, is nothing like what goes on in a hospital either. When I first arrived here, I was lost and confused. For about two weeks I had a nurse who actually talked to me."
Gina's blue eyes moistened.
"Neil is gone now. I don't know if he quit, or if they got rid of him. Anyway, he told me this place has four sections. They call them units. Each has seven patients. So, it can't be that big."

Kelly frowned. "That's only twenty eight patients. The way my nurses talked, I thought they had many more people to look after."

Looking at Kelly, Gina sighed. "We should try and bend that pipe before the doctor comes in here to see why we haven't."

Both women stared at the pipe, and it not only bent, but looked like invisible hands were tying it into a knot. Both women smiled, amazed by what they were doing. Neither knew how they were accomplishing the feat.

That thought had Kelly sending Gina another message, one mind to another.
"Do you think the drugs they force on us are giving us some kind of supernatural abilities. Or is it something more?"

Gina sighed. "I think it's more than just drugs. My memory has big holes in it. I can remember all kinds of things about life in general, but nothing about anything in my personal life."

Kelly also let out a small sigh.
"I'm the same way. I had a hard time even remembering my name. When I ask questions about my past or my family, I only get lame excuses. I wondered if the doctors here used some kind of hypnosis on us."

Gina grunted quietly.
"I don't much about hypnosis, but that sounds about right to me. All I want is to escape this place. I just can't come up with a way to do that."
This time, Kelly did start to nod. She stopped the motion quickly remembering that Doctor Mengle would be watching.

A moment later, he stepped in the room. Kelly held her breath, expecting him to ask what the two of them were doing.

Doctor Mengle didn't even bother looking at either woman. Instead, he rushed over to the counter and stared at the pipe. He finally turned back to face the women. Kelly stared at the man, thinking this was the first time she had seen an authentic smile on the man's face. She didn't like the look. Instead of comforting, the smile looked predatory.

The doctor's head was bobbing up and down. "Well done, well done. I think tonight, one more experiment will be enough. When I leave the room, I want the two of you to concentrate and straighten that pipe now."

Rubbing his hands together, the doctor hurried from the room. A moment after he left, his voice could be heard speaking.
"Okay, go ahead and begin."

While focusing on the pipe, Kelly still was able to send thoughts from her mind to Gina's.
"We have to find a way out. There isn't anyone inside this institute who will help us. We just have to find a way out ourselves. I'm afraid, once we do all the experiments the doctors want, or when we can't do something they ask, the people in this building will decide both you and I are expendable."

Giving one final push with her mind, Gina watched the pipe on the counter return to its' original shape. "I know you're right. I'll keep thinking of a way. I have a feeling you and I will be back in this room, or

another like it. Doctor Mengle will use every chance
he can to test what we can do."

Both woman stared straight ahead as Doctor Mengle
stepped in the room with another man.
Both pushed wheelchairs.
The doctor pointed toward the women, but turned to
the other man, who Kelly recognized as the intern,
who had called himself Scott..
"I'll take Miss Harris back to her room. You can
escort Miss Mitchell. Just make sure she gets to her
room. Miss Mitchell likes to defy orders."

The man nodded. "Don't worry Doctor Mengle, I'll
make sure she gets there and with no problems."

<u>*Chapter 9*</u>

In her room, Kelly was confused.

Although she was getting two shots a day of what she was told was Vitamin B, she hadn't been taken out of her room, since she had last been with Gina. After the two had stretched out and twisted the metal bar, Kelly had thought she and Gina would be forced to do experiments every night. She had no idea why the tests were stopped.

She had been given a change of clothing, which she was grateful for. Instead of the jeans and top, she had hoped for, she had been given a jogging outfit and another set of pajamas. Still, just having something besides pajamas to wear in the daytime, made her feel better, more normal.

With her mind cloudy from the drugs she was being given, Kelly wondered what the clothes might look like in reality. For all she knew, the clothing would actually be tattered and torn, if seen through drug free vision.

Right now, she didn't care, just thankful for even the smallest modifications.

Kelly was tired, more tired than she could remember being before. She was trying to keep her eyes open, even though she had just barely finished having her dinner, followed by the shot you hated.

She was hoping to be able to be awake, if she was finally taken to a room with Gina again.

Her heavy eyes closed. Kelly heard her name being spoken, but couldn't seem to open her eyes.
She answered anyway.
"Whose there? Doctor Mengle is that you?"

The male voice didn't answer her question. Kelly was certain it was the doctor though.
"Just relax Miss Mitchell. I have a few questions."

Kelly's head moved up and down slightly, the voice continued speaking.
"Tell me your name."

A slight grin appeared on Kelly's face, happy that she could answer the question.
"Kelly Mitchell."

The voice came back.
"Good, that's very good. Now can you tell me your address?"

Again Kelly nodded.
"Sure, I have a house in…"

The man interrupted Kelly's answer.
"No Kelly. You can't remember your address. You've had a head injury and your memory hasn't returned. These things take time, You need to have patience. Now, just repeat what I told you. Go ahead Kelly, answer me. Do you know your address?"

A frown appeared as Kelly shook her head.

"No, I can't remember my address. I had a head injury and my memory hasn't come back all the way yet. Hopefully, soon, my memories will return. I need to be patient."

Leaning toward Kelly, the man nodded.
"Good, very good. Now what about family? Can you remember your family?"
Again, as soon as Kelly started to nod, the man interrupted her.
"You can't remember your family either. Your memory hasn't returned. You can remember things about life in general, but nothing personal, no family, no address, is that right?"

The nod continued. "That's right. It's really strange. I have memories of life and how to do things, but nothing about my family, or anything in my personal life."

Kelly felt a hand patting her leg, before the man spoke again.
"Good Miss Mitchell, very good. Your memory of your personal past is an elusive thing. It may never return. You can deal with that. There's no need for you to try and search your mind right now. When the time is right, the memories will return. For now, you don't need those remembrances. Not knowing will not bother your other mental capabilities. Now, you are very tired. I'll just leave you alone to rest. You did well Kelly."

As the man said his last comment, Kelly could feel
her own pride swelling. She did well, the man had
told her so. She was satisfied by her performance.
All she wanted now was to rest. As the man left the
room, Kelly dropped into sleep.

When Kelly opened her eyes again, she felt rested.
She also knew she had been moved from her room.
She looked around from her position on a chair. She
was hoping to see Gina. She frowned, realizing right
now, she was alone. She heard the sound of a male
voice. She knew it was Doctor Mengle, and he
sounded surprising similar to the man she had talked
to, not long ago.

"Come on, Miss Harris. Quit dragging your feet. I
know you can move faster than that."

Kelly could hear the sound of Gina's voice and felt
relief the woman would be joining her.
"I'm coming, you don't have to drag me."

Looking toward the doorway, Kelly saw Doctor
Mengle roughly push Gina into the room.
"Go on, take your seat. We're running behind."

Gina walked toward where Kelly was seated, and sat
in the chair, situated just a few feet from her.
Kelly saw the woman was dressed in an outfit,
similar to her own.

Doctor Mengle leaned against the door frame and stared at both women.

"I expect both of you to follow orders and immediately. Do you understand me?"

Knowing better than to argue, both Kelly and Gina nodded. The doctor stepped over to the counter, grabbed something, then walked behind Kelly's chair. A moment later she felt a sharp stabbing pain. Moving from Kelly over to stand behind Gina, the doctor repeated the procedure. Gina jumped slightly at the stinging pain. The doctor then went back to the counter and lifted, either the cable that he had used previously, or one similar to it. Going behind the women, Doctor Mengle ran the cable from the back of Kelly's neck to the back of Gina's.

He moved toward the doorway. Turning he stared at both women.

"Tonight we will be trying something a bit different. I need to grab some things from the…"

A sound, like a shrill buzzer could be heard, coming from the speaker high up on the wall. It repeated three times before a voice was heard.

"Code three in Spruce Unit, Repeat, Code three in Spruce Unit."

After the announcement, the buzzer sounded three times again.

Kelly and Gina could see the terrified look on Doctor Mengle's face. He ran a hand over his face.

"Oh hell."

The doctor yelled toward the other room.
"Scott, get in here, now."

The man came running in. He was more terrified
than the doctor, who was extremely upset.
"You heard the announcement. Go and find Nurse
Parker or whoever is working tonight. Tell her
there's a code three. Let her know that she needs to
come take these two back to their rooms. As soon as
you do that, I want your ass down to the Spruce Unit.
We have trouble and will need all the help we can
get."

The man nodded and ran out of the room.
Doctor Mengle stared at Kelly and Gina.
"Nurse Parker will be here in a moment. I have to go.
Just sit there until she comes to get both of you.
Don't either of you move."

The doctor didn't expect or wait for a reply. Instead,
like Scott had, the doctor raced out of the room.

Kelly stared wide eyed at Gina. This time, with them
alone, Kelly didn't have to use her mind to speak.
Instead she opened her mouth, but was careful to
speak quietly.
"What's a code three?"

Gina shrugged. "I don't know. I never heard of that
before. Then again, our rooms don't have speakers in
them. It must be something serious for Doctor
Mengle to leave us in here waiting for the nurse."

Kelly nodded, then her eyes narrowed.
"Do you think we should try to escape? This might be the only chance we ever get."

Gina sighed. "I guess we better try. I have no idea how in the hell to get out of here. You're right though, this may be the only opportunity we get. We better take it."

Nodding, Kelly stood. "Let me get that stuff off your neck. I'll try not to hurt you."

Gina drew in a breath as Kelly stepped behind her.
She let the air out.
"Okay, I'm ready."

Lifting the long blonde hair off Gina's neck, Kelly pulled the cable off. Then, looking closer, she pulled out what looked like a small plug. With a disgusted look on her face, Kelly threw the thing across the room. She tried to stop the shudder that ran through her. She worried too much time was going by.
"Okay, I got it. Now, try and get that cable, and whatever it is hooked to, off me."

Gina stood. "Sit down and I'll see what I can do." Repeating what Kelly had just done, Gina also felt a revulsion seeing what had been embedded in Kelly's neck, knowing she had something similar in her own just moments earlier.

As soon as she felt the device being removed, Kelly
stood. She stared at Gina.
"Let's get out of here. Just keep your eyes open for
any people from the institute. Hide if you see anyone.
We need to find a stairway. I know this unit is on the
second floor."

Gina nodded. "Just stay close to me. I don't want to
be alone."

Reaching out, Kelly grabbed Gina's hand and held it
tight. She gave the slightly younger woman a smile.
"Don't worry, the two of us are doing this together.
Let's get the hell out of this loony bin."

Gina nodded. "I'm all for that."

The two women left the room. They tried to move
quickly, while staying slightly crouched down.
The two made their way along a hallway, lined with
several closed doors. Feeling Gina hesitate, Kelly
stared at the doors.
"I don't even want to know what's happening behind
those doors. Come on, keep moving. Look for some
kind of stairs."

Gina nodded and began walking more quickly.
Suddenly, she pulled back on Kelly's hand, seeing a
man running across the hallway. Both women leaned
back against the wall. Kelly felt like the room was
spinning. She knew she was feeling the effect of the
drugs. She blinked her eyes, hoping to fight off the

medication that had been forced on her, in order to get out of this surreal place. Kelly knew Gina must be experiencing the same thing. Staring at Gina, Kelly put a finger to her lips, warning the other woman they needed to stay quiet. Gina nodded she understood, and the two began moving again.

Reaching the end of the hall, they came to a crossroads, as another hallway hit the one they were in. Kelly turned to Gina and shrugged, as she whispered.
"Which way looks right?"
Shaking her head, Gina sighed. She looked both ways and then pointed to the right.
"That's the shorter of the halls. Let's try that."

Kelly smiled. "Okay with me. Just keep watching for anyone in a white coat."

Gina grunted out a quiet, half laugh.
"You don't have to remind me. If we get caught after trying this, I can't imagine what they'd do."

The two checked both ways, down the hall, then stepped out and began walking. Still holding hands, both women were still having problems keeping their balance. Neither knew how long until the drugs they had been given began to wear off.
Gina grabbed Kelly's hand so tight, Kelly thought it would break, she frowned as Gina whispered.
"Look, there's the stairway."

Looking in the direction Gina was, Kelly allowed herself a moment of hope, before nodding and moving toward the goal.

As the two started down the stairs, Gina let out a gasp. Her hand covered her mouth. Her voice was muffled as she spoke.
"Oh my hell, that's Scott, that intern. Oh no."

Also staring at the bottom of the stairs, Kelly saw what had Gina so upset. The man, who had been told by Doctor Mengle, to get to the Spruce Unit, was now obviously dead. His face was not only covered in blood, but it was the strange angle of his head, that told the horrific cause of his death. The man's neck was broken. Kelly's wide eyed, terrified look, matched Gina's. Kelly covered her mouth with her free hand, afraid she was going to be sick. Pulling her hand away, she shook her head.
"We need to get moving Gina. Don't look at him. Let's get down the stairs. Keep your eyes on the lookout for any institute people."

Gina nodded, even though looking away from the body was easier said than done. The two stepped down the stairs, staying to the edge the furthest from the body. At the bottom, they once again had to make a decision on which path to take.

The sound of men talking, made the decision for them.

Kelly pulled hard on Gina's hand and spoke quietly. "This way, let's get around the corner before those men get here."

Gina nodded and followed Kelly's lead. They arrived in another hallway. Kelly pointed at a door, too small to lead to a patient's room.
"Let's see what's in there. Maybe we can find a good hiding place."

The two hurried to the door and pulled it open, thankful it wasn't locked. Stepping inside, the two realized they were in a storage closet. They moved as far back as they could, and squatted down behind some buckets. Both held their breaths. They could hear the sound of male voices not far from their location.

"Shit, I can't believe this is happening. Scott is dead and who knows how many others?"

"You can blame Mengle for that. That bastard. Who in the hell let him bring death row inmates to the institute for him to experiment on? Something like this was bound to happen."

"At least Mengle was able to get that guy sedated. Did you hear the thud when that guy dropped?"

"What a frigging screw up. What I want to do, instead of heading to the other units, to make sure the patients are in their rooms, is to go out the door, head home, and never come back."

The voices faded as the men must have walked down the hall away from Gina and Kelly's hiding place. The two women were staring at each other in disbelief at what they had just heard.
Kelly whispered.
"Death row inmates? What the hell? I once thought this place was an actual hospital."
She shook her head.
"Can you believe that?"

Gina shrugged. "I thought the same. This place is like some kind of crazy, lunatic asylum."

Kelly nodded. "Yeah and the craziest people here are the doctors and nurses."
She stood up from her crouched position, then helped Gina to her feet as well.
"We need to find the door out of here. I think those guys must be gone. I can't hear them anymore."
Drawing in a deep breath, Gina nodded.

Going to the door, Kelly opened it an inch. Looking through the crack she had made, Kelly tried to peek out. Not seeing anything, she edged the door slowly an inch wider, then wider still. Finally, seeing no movement, she pushed the door all the way open. She grasped Gina's hand tightly.
"Come on, let's get out of this house of horrors."

The two walked through the institute. It seemed like they had walked miles, before both women came to a door. They stared at it for a long time, afraid to even hope it might be an exit. Kelly turned to Gina.
"What do you think? Should we try it?"

With a shrug, Kelly then nodded.
"It's worth taking a look. Not only do we have to worry about the people that work here finding us, but whoever left Scott lying dead on the stairs could also be running around."

Reaching forward, Kelly held her breath and turned the doorknob. Pushing it away from her, she saw darkness. She knew it must still be night outside. She pushed the door further, and felt slightly cooler air coming in. Turning to Gina, she smiled.
"It leads outside. Come on, let's make a run for it."

Stepping outside, the two were almost in shock. Neither had been outside for a long time. For Gina it had been months, for Kelly, although a shorter time, it felt like it had been eternity. The women could see the pine trees not far from where they stood.
Kelly pointed. "We can hide out there. Let's get away from this building, then we can try to come up with a plan."

Nodding her agreement, Gina followed just inches behind Kelly, as the pair headed into the trees.
Gina was frowning.
"How will we know which way to go?"

Kelly shrugged. "Right now, I just want to put some distance between us and the institute. By now, they probably have checked our rooms, and found them empty. I'm sure they'll be out looking for us. We need to find a good place to hide, but like I said, I want to get away from this building first."

The two women began hiking. They walked a block into the woods, then turned to the right, and began walking again. Kelly pointed back through the woods they had just walked through.
"I think I can see headlights. There must be a road not far from here."

Kelly nodded. "Just as long as it heads away from Pine View, and not back toward it, I'm happy."

Kelly and Gina walked about what seemed like two city blocks distance, when they saw a tree surrounded by taller bushes. Kelly pointed.
"Let's go head in those bushes and try to come up with some kind of plan."

Gina nodded, and the two moved to the area. Pushing aside a few branches on the bushes, the two ducked beneath the vegetation. They sat quietly for several minutes, just trying to make sense of the strange night they had just endured.

Kelly was frowning. "I can't believe we got out of that place. Do you think what we heard those men saying was true? Would Doctor Mengle actually be doing experiments on death row inmates?"

Gina shrugged. "Why not? Look what he did to us. I doubt if that man cares who he does things to. As long as he feels he is getting results, I think he'd experiment on his own family."

Kelly sighed. "I hate to even think that could be true, but know you are probably right. What I can't understand is everybody else in that place going along with his atrocious works. Why hasn't anyone tried to stop all that?"

Gina shook her head. "I imagine they want to keep their jobs. Or maybe they're afraid they'll become a part of the experiments themselves."

Gina yawned after she spoke, and Kelly frowned. "Are you tired?"

Gina nodded. "Right now, I'm tired, confused and scared to death."

Kelly nodded. "I feel the same. We both need sleep. I think we need to get further away from the institute though. Do you think you can walk?"

With a shrug, Gina then nodded.
"I can walk, but how do we even know where we are going? What if we get twisted around in these woods and end up back at the place?"

Kelly shook her head.
"I don't think that will happen. We walked into the woods behind the institute then turned and walked away from the area. I can still see some headlights not far from here. I think if we keep walking in the woods this direction, we'll be moving parallel to that road. Let's keep hiking this way. If we can get even another half a mile away, I'd feel a lot better. Once we do that, we can find another hiding place where both of us can get some rest."

Looking at Kelly, Gina frowned.
"What then?"

Shaking her head, Kelly shrugged.
"I don't know. I hope we can find a town close by. Maybe find a police station where we can get some help. We know our names, but not much else. I'm hoping the police might have received some kind of missing persons reports on us. During one of my flashbacks, I think my mom was in the room with me."
Kelly sighed and his voice trembled as she continued speaking.
"I also saw two men kidnap me. They threw me in a car when I was out jogging. I couldn't tell where I was. I hope as these drugs wear off, more and more of my past recollections will return."

Gina nodded. "I've experienced some of those types of episodes. Is that what they are called, flashbacks?"

Kelly laughed lightly and was surprised how good it felt. She then nodded.
"They're called flashbacks in my mind, and that's good enough for me."

Gina smiled. "That's good enough for me. I hope I start having more flashbacks as the time goes on as well. No one should be allowed to do what the institute did to us."
Gina stood. "Let's get moving before I give up and fall asleep right here."

Getting to her own feet, Kelly nodded.
"Best plan I've heard in a long time. Let's go."

Chapter 10

Kelly was the first to wake. She stared around her, confused. Then, the nights events flooded into her mind. Drawing in a deep breath, she looked over at Gina, still asleep. Hating to wake the younger woman, Kelly knew neither of them had much in the way of options.
Reaching over, Kelly shook Gina's shoulder.
"Gina, it's Kelly. Wake up Gina. We need to get moving."

The blue eyes opened. Gina frowned as she covered the yawn that hit. She too was trying to get oriented to the strange surroundings. She and Kelly were beneath thick bushes. Gina could just barely see light filtering into the darkness of their concealment.
"Where are we?"

Shaking her head, Kelly shrugged.
"I'm not sure. When we stopped to rest, my best guess is we were a mile from the institute. The sun is out now, I think we should start moving again."

Rubbing her stomach, Gina frowned.
"I'm starving. We walked more last night than I have in months. No wonder we were so tired. That and the stress of trying to escape crazy doctors, and a death row inmate, on a killing spree."

Kelly nodded. "I feel like I'm still in a nightmare and should be waking up to reality some time soon."

Gina grunted. "I wish that was the case. Sadly we are both awake and this nightmare hasn't ended yet."

Kelly shrugged. "At least we are away from the institute and Doctors Strange and Stranger. Now, if we can find a town with a police station, maybe the rest of the nightmare can end."

Although not as positive as Kelly, Gina knew the woman was right. She smiled.
"I hate that either of us went through all of this, but I'm so thankful you are with me. I don't think I would have even tried escaping on my own"

Kelly nodded and grasped Gina's hand. She tightened her grip on it a moment before letting go.
"I feel the same way about you."
Kelly sighed. "I guess it's time for the two of us to do a bit of hiking."

Gina frowned. "Do you have any idea which way to go?"

With a grin, Kelly pointed at a large pine tree that looked like it had been hit by lightning some time in the not too distant past.
"When we crawled under these bushes, I looked around to orient myself. That tree is in line with the route we were headed. If we head that way, we will be heading further from Pine View."

Kelly nodded. "Exactly the direction I want to be in."

The two woman began walking. They stayed far enough in the trees that no one could see them, but close enough to hear traffic, running on the road, that ran parallel to them.

As the two walked, they talked about different things, but neither had the memory they needed. The one allowing either to share anything about their past lives. Still, both had recollections of television shows, and movies, they had seen. Neither woman knew where they had been when they had watched the shows, or if they had been with friends, or family when they did. They found they had things in common, that is if, their own memories could be trusted. Kelly explained to Gina about being hypnotized.

Gina nodded. "I wondered if the doctors were using more than drugs. I thought there had to be something else. I don't remember much, but I can't imagine retaining some memories, and not others, because of the drugs. I just hope both of us continue having flashbacks of the past so we can piece our lives together."

The two were walking better in the light of day and as the medications slowly wore off. Kelly figured they were walking at least two miles an hour. By the time the sun rose high above and then began

descending behind the trees, which were keeping the women cool, Kelly guessed they had walked fifteen or twenty miles. She pointed in the direction they knew the road to be.
"Look, a house. I see another one just up the way. I think we are getting closer to a town."

Light blue eyes lit up, as Gina ran a hand through her long blonde hair.
"Oh my gosh, I think you're right."
Then she frowned. "Do you think we're far enough away from the institute to be safe?"

Kelly shrugged, her own light brown eyes, were darkened with worry.
"I can only say, I hope so. We have no guarantees, but anything is better than where we were."

Kelly grunted. "Unless someone tries to take us back, that is."

Shaking her head, Kelly's eyes narrowed.
"Not this time. If they try, I'll do anything, and everything, I can to stop that from happening."

The two began walking again, noticing more and more houses, tucked in here and there, in the thinning forest. Kelly was grateful the two of them hadn't ended up in the thick woods that she had seen from her room window, when she had been in the institute. Right now the two of them were tired, thirsty and hungry. Kelly was certain if they had gone deeper into those woods, they wouldn't have survived.

She pointed toward the noise of cars.

"Let's get closer to the road, maybe we'll see a sign or two so we can know where we are."

Gina nodded and the two moved closer to the road, without getting close enough for someone in a car passing by, to see them.

They had walked another mile when Gina pointed.

"Look at that, oh my gosh. I can't believe it."

Looking up, Kelly smiled in disbelief at the sign on the edge of the road. She read the words aloud.

"Welcome to Westbend. Enjoy your stay."

A smile also curled up the edges of Gina's mouth.

"I never thought we'd actually find a town."

She turned to Kelly and laughed.

"Thanks for being the navigator. I would have gotten totally lost."

Kelly gave Gina a slight bow. Just finding a town made her feel giddy.

"My pleasure, now the next step. Watch for a police station."

Gina nodded, but frowned.

"Do we look okay for walking out in a town in public."

She brushed her hands over the legs of her sweatpants, trying to knock off dried mud and pine needles.

Frowning, Kelly pointed at Gina.
"Turn around, I'll check your clothes, then you can look at mine."

After the two made themselves a bit more presentable, they walked into the Westbend city limits.

The pair walked four blocks before they saw a sign that said 'police station', followed by a white arrow that pointed to the right. They turned in the direction the arrow pointed, and began walking.
Both Gina and Kelly could see the building the moment they turned the corner. It was a two level building. That made it one story higher than most of the places nearby.
The two walked faster, unable to stop the grins that appeared on their dirty, tired, faces.
Both women also had a trace of fear hovering in the backs of their minds. Unsure of what they might find in the police station. Would those inside be friend or foe? Faced with the idea someone could be working with the institute, even this far away, the women both knew they didn't have much choice, but to go inside.

They stepped together into the station. Both stared at a man who sat alone in the large, front room.

He looked up as they walked toward him, his dark eyes held curiosity. To him, both the women who entered, looked like they had spent the night in the woods.
"Can I help you?"

Taking Gina's hand, Kelly pulled her friend with her, as she stepped forward.
"We need help. The two of us just escaped from Pine View Institute."

Hearing the name of a place he hated, Frank Whitley stared at the women. He ran a hand through his almost black hair, before frowning.
He pointed at chairs across the desk from him.
"Sit down here. I'm Deputy Frank Whitley. I'll need some information."
When Kelly and Gina took their seats, Frank leaned over the desk, his dark brown eyes narrowed, staring at the women, as he whispered.
"Don't ever mention the name of that place again. Not in the walls of this station anyway."
He leaned back, hoping the two wouldn't ask him why.

Both women frowned, but also had a feeling about the reasoning behind the deputy's strange comment. It seemed as if they would never get far enough away from Pine View Institute to escape it's dark influence.
Kelly and Gina nodded their understanding.

Sitting back, Frank tried to give the women a reassuring grin. Then he sighed and pulled a notebook over in front of him.
"Now, I'll need your names."

Kelly looked at Gina. "You can go first."

Gina nodded. "My name is Gina Harris."

Frank wrote down the name, then frowned.
"Can you give me your address?"
When Gina shook her head, tears stood in her eyes.
Frank sighed, but nodded.
"That's okay Gina. We'll figure that out later."
He turned to Kelly. "And your name?"

A hint of a smile crossed Kelly's face, as she allowed a ray of hope to enter her heart. This man seemed to understand their predicament, even if he wasn't stating that.
"I'm Kelly, Kelly Mitchell."

The deputy nodded, and wrote down the name.
"That's good. I'm guessing the two of you could use a drink of water."

Nods by both women, had Frank standing and walking to a small refrigerator that sat in the back of the room. As he walked back, carrying two bottles, another man stepped in the room.
The guy was over six feet tall and carried at least twenty extra pounds on his frame. His blonde hair

was cut so short, it was almost non-existent. His brown eyes stared harshly at the women, before he turned to look at Frank.

"Is there something I can help you with deputy?"

Frank shook his head.

"No, but thanks Sheriff Bertram. I'll be heading out with these two in a minute. It's a domestic dispute. They're having a problem getting some personal items from an ex-roommate."

Brown eyes frowned, and narrowed, but the man only nodded.

"If you leave, get Marna to sit at the desk. I have to take off myself. They've had some trouble over at the institute."

Hearing what the sheriff said, Kelly and Gina tried not to show any emotions. Both had similar feelings that the sheriff wouldn't be on their side. Nor care about what they had gone through, and were still dealing with.

When the sheriff turned and walked out the door, both women let out a sigh of relief.

Watching them, Frank was glad the two had realized why he had asked them not to mention the institute. Frank set the water bottles in front of the women.

"Just relax here a minute. I'll go ask Marna to come watch the desk."

When Frank walked away, Kelly and Gina quickly
opened the bottles and gulped down large drinks.
Kelly frowned watching Gina almost drain the whole
bottle. She reached over and pushed the bottle gently
away from Gina's mouth.
"Take it easy. If you drink to much right now, that
water is going to come back up."

Nodding, Gina smiled. "Thanks Kelly. I knew that,
but was just so damn thirsty."
Then she frowned. "I don't trust that sheriff. Did you
see that angry look he gave us?"

Kelly nodded. "You couldn't miss it. I'm just glad he
left. He said they had a problem at the institute. We
know what that means, I think Deputy Whitley is
going to help us though."
Kelly ran a hand through her short, brown hair and
let out a breath.
"I'm just glad we didn't run into that sheriff first. He
said he was going to the institute. We would have
been in for a world of hurt, if he knew what we did,
and took us back there."

Blue eyes wide, Gina nodded.
"Oh hell, ain't that the truth?"

The women looked up, as Frank came back in the
room, followed by a woman with long, red hair and
gentle, green eyes. Both Kelly and Gina were
relieved to see a compassionate look in the emerald
eyes. The woman smiled.

"I'm Marna. Frank tells me the two of you need help.
I want to tell you that you're not the first ones who
have landed in the predicament you're in. I hope
you're the last though. The two of you just listen to
Frank. He knows what he's doing and you can trust
him."

Gina and Kelly stared at the woman as she took the
seat Frank had been in. Kelly spoke for both of them.
"That's some good information to hear. Gina and I
both feel like we escaped the worst stages of hell.
It's just nice to see a couple of friendly faces for a
change."

Marna smiled. "Thanks, I was hoping you would see
that Frank and I wouldn't hurt you."
She turned to look up at Frank.
"Well, what you waiting for? Take these two and get
them some help."

Frank laughed and shook his head.
"A bit bossy today aren't you Marna?"

Marna shrugged and then laughed.
"Hell Frank, I'm a bit bossy every day. Go on, get
out of here. I can handle things."

Motioning at the women, Frank smiled.
"Okay, the three of us are going to take a little ride."
Seeing the matching frown lines that ran across the
women's brows, Frank shook his head.

"Don't worry, we'll be headed the opposite direction that Pine View lies in."

Standing, Kelly and Gina nodded. They turned to smile their gratitude at Marna, before following Frank out of the building.

The deputy walked over to a patrol car. He turned to look at Kelly and Gina.
"I'm sorry to make you ride in a police vehicle. The two of you will also have to sit in back. Sorry about that too. We only have to drive about a half mile and then the two of you can get out and relax."

Putting their trust in the man and his words, the two took seats in the back of the car. Frank got in the front seat and started the car. He pulled away from the station and began talking quickly.
"I'm taking you to meet a friend of mine. You can trust her. Her name is Elizabeth Hillyard, but everyone calls her Liz, and she wouldn't have it any other way. Liz knows all about Pine View Institute. The two of you wouldn't be the first ones she has helped. I'm going to have to leave you both there and get back to the station. I'll be running your names through the system. I'm sure someone has put in a missing persons report."

In the backseat, Kelly was frowning.
"We appreciate that, you'll never know how much. I was told by the nurses at the institute that might have already been done."

Kelly sighed. "I never actually believed what they said. Trusting anyone at the institute, is like hoping a mountain could fly."
Kelly frowned. She had heard someone say that before. She tried to think who, but the memory floated away. She shook her head with disgust and despair.

Looking in the rear view mirror, Frank recognized the look on Kelly's face.
"I heard that saying with pigs, not mountains. You must have heard it differently. Don't try too hard to remember. Forcing a memory will just make you frustrated. Have faith that Liz can help with that."
A grin sat on the deputy's face. Kelly could see it in the reflection in the mirror. She smiled back, hoping Frank was right.

The women felt the car slowing down and looked eagerly, but anxiously, out the window.
Frank turned the patrol vehicle into the driveway of a large, two story, older home. The building was a light yellow color, with white trim. The bushes, trees and grass were well manicured.
The place looked inviting.
Frank cleared his throat and spoke.
"Welcome to Hillyard Haven. Come on, let's introduce the two of you to the owner."

Getting out of the car, Kelly and Gina stared at the house. A feeling of relief, and peace, seemed to wash over the two. Kelly turned to Gina and smiled, her

light brown eyes sparkled. She slid a hand through
Gina's elbow.
"I think things are looking much better."

Gina nodded, lifted her hand and crossed her fingers.
"Here's hoping for the best."

The two followed Frank to the cement steps, covered
with a blue carpet runner. They walked up to the
door where Frank knocked.

A moment later the door opened wide. A heavy set
woman, in her forties, with short brown hair that had
blonde streaks running through it, stared at Frank.
She had a large smile on her face.
"Frank, how are you? I was kind of expecting you to
show up on my doorstep today. Your handsome face
has been floating around in my mind all morning.
That happens sometimes."

Frank laughed. "Oh Liz, thanks for calling my face
handsome. I bet that's something you say that to all
the men."

Shaking her head, Liz frowned.
"Oh, not to all the men. I know a few who would
definitely not get a compliment from me."
Liz looked at the two women standing just behind
Frank, almost hiding.
"Do you want to introduce me to your friends,
Frank?"

He nodded. "Since they are the ones that have me standing here, I better. Elizabeth Hillyard, meet Kelly Mitchell and Gina Harris."
Frank pointed at each woman as he said their name. Then he spoke again.
"If you haven't guessed by now, these two recently fled Pine View Institute."

Liz sighed heavily and shook her head with disgust. She stared at the women for a moment, her cerulean blue eyes filled with a mix of emotions. Her compassion for the women was accompanied by her anger at the place Frank had just mentioned.
"When are you going to shut down that house of horrors Frank?"

Shrugging, Frank shook his head.
"Not until I can rip the badge off the sheriff's chest. You know that jerk is on Pine View's payroll. He's up at that place right now. He said they had problems up there. I haven't got any details yet, but you know it's something horrible, if that place is involved."

Liz sighed, but nodded.
"Sadly, I do know that. Never mind that for now, all of you come on in."
She stared at Kelly, then Gina.
"I'm sorry for what I know you must have gone through."

Moving back, Frank motioned for the women to step in the house, but he shook his head at Liz's invite.

"I need to get back to the station."
He turned to Kelly and Gina.
"You're in good hands here. Liz knows what to do."

Liz nodded. "That I do. I also have a room for the
two of you to stay while we get everything
straightened out."

Looking at Liz, then at the two women he had
brought to her, Frank smiled.
"I'll be back when my shift is over. I haven't gotten
to hear the story of how these women got out of that
place yet."

Liz clapped her hands together.
"Great, the ladies here and I can make you dinner. I
know how you bachelors are about eating a good,
healthy meal."

As Frank laughed, Kelly stared at his face and
realized that Liz had been right, the man was quite
handsome, especially when he smiled. He reminded
her of someone she had seen before, but with her
brain so foggy, she couldn't think of who it might be.
Kelly thought maybe an actor she might have seen
somewhere. Maybe in the old magazine she'd
reluctantly been allowed to have at the institute.
Kelly and Gina said their good-byes to Frank, while
also letting him know how grateful they were to him,
before they let him leave.

After the three women had watched Frank back out of the driveway and drive away, Liz opened the front door wider.

"You two, get on in here. First I want to hear your story of escape. Then, I'll explain to you how I can help fix what that bastard Mengle did."

Seeing the shock in Kelly and Gina's eyes, Liz laughed.

"I don't know if those wide eyed expressions are because of my language, or your surprise at me knowing about the doctor. We'll sort through things and figure it all out soon enough."

Liz frowned.

"I think we should do our talking in the kitchen. I imagine the two of you are starving."

The pair nodded and followed the woman through the house. The place was as meticulously neat on the inside, as on the out.

The two women had the same conflicting emotions. Nervousness at what might be ahead, and hope that they might somehow get their lives back.

Chapter 11

In the kitchen, Kelly and Gina were asked to take seats, while Liz began digging through the large, double door, refrigerator that covered a quarter of one wall in the room.
Liz laughed as she placed plate, after plate, of food on the table.
"I'm going to bring the food to you today, but after that, you'll be doing your own meal preparation."

The two women smiled and nodded. Both had already decided they liked Elizabeth Hillyard.
They had looked around the room, loving the cozy feeling the cedar wood cupboards against the magenta walls created.

Once all the food was on the table and Liz had gotten the two women plates, utensils and a drink, she sat down to join them.
"Go ahead and eat. I'll talk, when you two are finished eating, I want to hear whatever you can remember."
Waiting until after the two women began eating, Liz then began speaking.
"First of all, you should know, the two of you aren't the only people I have helped who came out of the institute. The first was twenty years ago when I first graduated from college. The last was just six months ago. People seldom get away from that hideous place. I'm just happy to help those who come my way."
Liz thought for a moment before continuing.

"I should give you some background on Pine View Institute. That place was once a summer retreat for an affluent family. That was well before I was born. Hell, it was probably before my parents were born. I'm sure the two of you never saw the actual building. If you were to drive down the main road, you might be able to get a glimpse of the front of the place, but not much more. When the government bought the building, back in the fifties, they built the institute behind the original home. Hiding their dirty secrets from prying eyes. Walking behind the facade, you would see a two story building that holds over twenty patients."

Shaking her head in disgust, Liz took a drink, before continuing.

"Patients is the wrong word to use in association with that abhorrent place.The experiments that go on in the institute are detestable. Sadly, our government is always looking for a new weapon to use against those they consider enemies. There are even people in this town who look the other way or who are willing to take money to further those interests. Two of the people I was able to help, had been introduced to me by way of the emergency room of the hospital here in town. My biggest fear is to find the destruction done by the doctors up there can't be reversed."

Liz sighed and shook her head. She frowned as she stared at the women.

"Do you need something more to eat or drink?"

Both women shook their heads vehemently.

Making Liz smile and nod.

"Doctor Mengle, and his associate, Doctor Anders, remind me of the cowards who called themselves doctors during the atrocities committed during world war two. Doctor Mengle's favorite heinous act is playing with the mind. Something our own government also seems fascinated with."

Across from Liz, the two women let out a simultaneous gasp. Liz nodded.
"I know the two of you suffered from what the doctor finds almost an amusing pastime. You should know I am a trained hypnotherapist, and I work in holistic medicine. I believe I can help you to recover what that monster stole from you."
Liz could see sadness, but also a ray of hope, shining in the eyes staring at her. She nodded.
"Like said, I have helped others. Not just those who escaped from the institute, but many others."
Seeing the two women had pushed their plates away. Liz leaned forward.
"Your turn now. If you can just give me the basics of your experience for now, we can delve deeper into it all, in the days to come. When we finish, we can find the two of you some clothes. I have compiled a large selection over the years. People come and go, but I keep any extra clothing in a spare room. I just never know who might end up on my doorstep. I also would make a bet the two of you would like a nice shower or a hot bath."

Both women nodded at the idea. Kelly turned to look at Gina.

"You were at the institute longer than I was. I think you should tell Liz your story first."

A frown line ran across Gina's forehead. Her light blue eyes widened, but she nodded and cleared her throat. She was having a hard time keeping eye contact with Liz as she spoke. Instead her fingers nervously drew circles on the table in front of her. "I guess I was at the institute for about three months."
A shrug of her shoulders, was followed by a sigh. "I don't know how I got there. I didn't even remember my name at first. I was given drugs. I don't know if I was hypnotized, but think I was."
A sob escaped as Gina shook her head.
"They stole my memories. Damn it, they had no reason, permission or authority to do that."
A hand came up to first, cover Gina's mouth, then to wipe her face.
"I'm sorry, it's hard to think about all this."
Gina drew in a deep breath.
"Later, Doctor Mengle used Kelly and I together for his experiments. He had us using our minds to bend metal and start fires. I'm guessing that's what you meant when you said the government wants new weapons."

Liz nodded. "Sadly, yes. How did you and Kelly get away?"

Turning to look at Kelly, Gina then returned her gaze to Liz. She recalled all she could about the night the two had escaped. Her voice shook as she talked about the death row inmate killing the man she thought was an intern, or something similar. The she repeated the conversation she and Kelly had overheard while they hid in the closet.

Kelly was nodding. "The men we could hear, blamed Mengle. So, even those working in that place know what is going on. They can't claim they were ignorant to the truth."

Liz also nodded. "That's true, they will claim they were following orders. A damn, lame excuse. Sadly one used a lot in times of war. Anyway, like I said, even a few people in town are on the payroll. That includes Sheriff Bertram."
She shook her head.
"We can talk about all that in the days ahead. Right now Kelly, I'd like to hear what you know."

The sound of a harsh laugh, grunted out, could be heard, before Kelly began speaking.
"I don't even know when I arrived at the institute. When I woke, I was told I had been asleep a week. But, who knows, the whole place was filled with liars. I do remember being hypnotized, or at least that's what I thought Doctor Mengle was doing. I know he asked my address and I started to answer, but he interrupted me and said I couldn't remember."
Kelly sighed, she felt like crying.
"And he was right, I couldn't remember that or anything personal about my life. I can't figure out

how Gina and I were able to do the things the doctor had us do."

Liz nodded. "The mind is a mysterious place and shouldn't have evil people like those at the institute messing with it. I hope to fix the wrongs they did, but that can wait until tomorrow. If the two of you are done eating, why don't we find you those clothes I mentioned? Then you can both get cleaned up if you want."

Both Gina and Kelly stared at Liz, amazed at her generosity. Kelly spoke for both of them.
"I don't know how either of us can repay your kindness. Some day, when all of this is hopefully behind us, I plan on finding a way."

Gina nodded. "That goes for me too. Right now, I don't have a penny to my name, or none I am aware of. But, I won't let your generosity go without a payback when I can."

Standing, Liz shook her head.
"All I want right now, is for the two of you to feel comfortable here, and get your lives straightened around."

Kelly sighed. "At least let us clean up this mess we made."

Liz laughed. "Let's get you both cleaned up first. This kitchen has seen worse. Come on, I'll show you where to find the clothes, the bathroom, and where you can sleep tonight. After that's all done, we can decide what we'll be making Frank for dinner. I know his shift ends at five. He'll be here shortly after that."

Going upstairs in the house, Kelly and Gina were taken to a room that held an enormous quantity of a variety of clothing. Liz let them find a couple of changes of clothing, before showing the two women the room they would be sharing, and the bathroom that was theirs to use as well. Gina took the first shower, followed by Kelly.
When they finished getting themselves washed up, the two went down to the kitchen to help Liz straighten the room.

The three talked as they worked, getting to know each other. Kelly had asked Liz about the beautiful landscaping outside.

Liz had smiled. "I helped a young man with a problem. He owns a landscaping company and maintains my yard as payment."
Liz laughed. "I helped him over five years ago. I'm sure I owe him much more for his work, than he ever owed me for mine, but he won't accept any payment."
Liz shrugged.
"Well, I shouldn't say that. Bryce does allow me to cook him a meal once or twice a week. The two of you will be meeting him in a day or two, I'm sure."

After cleaning, the three sat at the table to decide on the evening meal. They decided to make spaghetti, garlic bread, and a salad to share with Frank when he arrived. Sharing the preparation of the meal, the three were able to get the meal done just minutes before they heard the sound of the doorbell.

Looking at Kelly and Gina, Liz smiled.
"That will be Frank. Why don't you two start setting the table, while I let him in?"
Glad to be doing something helpful, both nodded their agreement at the suggestion.

Liz came back a moment later, with Frank following her. He was smiling and rubbing his hands together.
"Oh wow, it smells great in here. I really appreciate the three of you putting together a home cooked meal for me."

Liz grunted. "Frank, you need one. I know you must live on microwave dinners."

Frank laughed and shrugged.
"That or sandwiches. I know how to cook a few things. It's not worth the work to make a meal for just one person to eat."

Pointing at the table, Liz nodded.
"Everything's ready. Why doesn't everyone take a seat? I'll just say a quick blessing on the food and then everyone can dig in."

Heads bowed, after the group sat down. As soon as they all echoed the 'Amen' after Liz, the only sound in the room was that of people grabbing the food, and filling their plates.

While they ate, Liz, Kelly and Gina, filled Frank in on the rest of the story he hadn't gotten the chance to hear earlier.

When they finished talking, Frank shook his head. "That place is an abomination. One of these days, I'm going to find a way to get the doors shuttered. When Sheriff Bertram returned from the institute he told me that one of the patients had died, along with two others who worked there. I don't know how the patient got loose, but he did some damage in the short time he was free from his captivity. The sheriff didn't say, but I'm sure Doctor Mengle killed the patient."

Kelly's light brown eyes widened, as she stared at Frank.

"We heard two men talking. They said the doctor gave that man some kind of shot and he dropped to the floor."

Frank nodded. "I'm sure the shot they were talking about was what killed the man."

Leaning back, Frank patted his stomach.

He looked at Liz.

"If you keep offering to feed me, I won't be able to fit into my uniform anymore."

Liz laughed. "I doubt that. You spend all your free
time in your backyard chopping wood."
She rolled her eyes.
"Then you give half of that away."

Frank shrugged. "I like chopping wood. I can't use
all I chop and there are a lot of people in town who
can't go haul wood for their stoves. I'm just happy to
be able to help them out."

Across the table from Frank, Kelly was staring at
him. Her eyes lit up and she blurted out a name.
"Sidney Poitier."

Frank frowned. "What?"

Kelly shook her head.
"Sorry, I've been wondering who you remind me of.
My memory is so sketchy. I vaguely remember
watching this movie. It was an old show."
Kelly frowned, thinking. Then she smiled as one
evasive memory finally came to her.
"Guess who's coming to dinner. That's what it was
called. You remind me of the actor in that show."

Beside Kelly, Liz was nodding.
"She's right Frank. You do look like him. When he
was younger of course."

Frank rolled his eyes.

"You better say when he was younger. I'm only thirty five."
He turned to look at Kelly.
"Thanks though. I consider that a compliment. I was sad when I heard he had passed away. Such a great actor."

Kelly was frowning, she didn't remember the actor had passed away. Then again, there was so much she couldn't recollect.
"I didn't know he had passed away. Such an amazing actor. It's funny that I can remember watching television shows and movies, but not if I watched them with someone or not."

Nodding, Gina sighed.
"I'm that way too. My memory reminds me of that colander we used to drain the spaghetti with tonight."

Running a hand through her hair, Liz smiled, looking from one woman's face to the other.
"Starting tomorrow, we're going to see if we can fix that. The process isn't something that can be done in one day though. I'm afraid both of you are going to need some patience."

Frank nodded. "While Liz helps the two of you, I'll be busy digging through police reports to find anything related to both of you. I have no idea where either of you lived before all this happened."

Kelly sighed. "If we're lucky, Gina and I will be able to remember more after our sessions with Liz."

All agreed with Kelly's sentiment. Soon after, they worked together to once again straighten the kitchen. As she worked, Kelly kept glancing at Frank. The man really was attractive. She hoped no one noticed her studying him.

Liz, who was watching, had a large grin on her face. She wondered if she could play matchmaker, along with all the other things she was doing?

<u>*Chapter 12*</u>

For the first time since Gina and Kelly had found themselves prisoners in the Pine View Institute, both women slept well. They were slightly disoriented when they awoke, but it only took a few moments before both had large smiles on their faces.

Liz appeared in the doorway of the bedroom.
"Good morning. Glad to see you are both up. I hope the two of you slept well. I have the coffee on, and some breakfast ready, if the two of you are hungry. Come on down to the kitchen when you're ready."

Gina and Kelly got out of the beds, that sat close to each other in the same room. They had been glad when they had been told the two of them would be sleeping in the same room.
After their frightening ordeal, neither wanted to be alone. They dressed in the clothes Liz had given them, washed up and headed downstairs.
The kitchen smelled like fresh baked biscuits.
Gina lifted her head and sniffed the air.
"Something smells wonderful."

Looking at the two women, Liz smiled.
"I made biscuits. Grab a cup of coffee, and sit down. I also have eggs, and sausage, if you'd like some."

Kelly frowned. "I think I'll just have coffee and a biscuit. My stomach is doing cartwheels. I have to admit, I'm a bit nervous about the sessions we'll be having today."

Staring at her, Liz's blue eyes filled with compassion. Looking at the woman, who had taken her and Gina into her home, Kelly loved the expressive look in the intense blue eyes. They sparkled like sapphires, when Liz smiled.
"No need to be nervous. I have to tell you though, it may take a few sessions to undue whatever damage Mengle placed on you and Gina."

Gina frowned at Liz's comment. She had been hoping, after just one session, all would be back to normal. She didn't know much about the inner workings of the mind, and had to accept what Liz was saying. The woman was a professional and it was apparent to see, a compassionate soul.
Gina and Kelly grabbed their coffee and a biscuit, then took a seat at the table.

Liz joined the pair. She glanced at each of their faces a moment, before speaking.
"I want to do these sessions individually. You two can decide who goes first. While I hold the first session, whoever is not in the room, will have to find something to keep you occupied. I have a room filled with books and games. There's also a TV in the living room. I'd have you go out into the yard, but until we learn if Mengle or one of his goons might be looking for you, I feel it's best to stay hidden up."

Kelly and Gina exchanged worried glances, neither had thought much about people from the institute hunting for them. Gina brushed a hand nervously through her long hair.
"Oh hell."
She turned to look at Liz.
"Do you really think they would do that?"

Liz shrugged. "The honest answer is, I don't know. I'd rather be safe than sorry, though. Until Frank gets more information about what's happening up at the institute, I want both of you in here where I can keep an eye on you. Try not to worry about any of that right now. Just finish up your breakfast and we can get started."

After having a drink of her coffee, Kelly turned to look at Gina.
"You can have the first session. You spent a lot more time at the awful place than I did. I think I'll go watch some television if that's okay? Maybe I'll see something to trigger my memories."

Setting her own cup down, Liz nodded.
"That's actually a good idea. You never know when even one little thing you see, can start an avalanche of thoughts."
Picking up her cup, Liz took the last drink and then stood. She walked to the sink, rinsed her cup and turned to look at Gina.
"Just let me know when you're ready to start. We'll be going in my office. The room is just on the side of

the living room. If Kelly is in there watching
television, the three of us will just be steps away
from each other."

Finishing her own coffee, Gina also stood and rinsed
the cup before turning to Liz, with a shrug.
"I'm about as ready as I'll ever be."

Stepping over to the younger woman, Liz slid an arm
around her shoulders.
"You're going to do fine Gina. I'll explain every
thing step by step as we go through the session. I'll
do all I can to fix what those jerks at the institute did.
Hopefully soon, you'll be back with your family, and
friends. Then this nightmare will be over."

Gina nodded, even though she wasn't even half as
sure about what might happen. She knew she had to
put her trust in Liz. She also felt, in her heart, that
was the right thing to do.

Liz turned to Kelly. "You can walk with us. I'll get
the TV turned on for you."

A short time later, Kelly was on the couch, watching
a twenty four hour news station, hoping to see
something familiar. While she stared at the screen,
Liz and Gina were in Liz's office.

Instead of having Gina sit on the couch in the room,
Liz instead placed two chairs face to face, and had
Gina sit in front of her. The two were close enough

their knees were just a whisper away from making contact. Liz reached out her hands for Gina to take. Gina gratefully slipped her hands into Liz's.

The older woman stared into the younger woman's light blue eyes.
"I want you to close your eyes Gina. Just relax. You're safe here. Close your eyes and relax. I'm going to count backwards. I'll start at one hundred, when I reach seventy five, I want you to continue the count. Go slow and easy. When I let go of your hands, you will be asleep, but able to hear my voice and answer me. Do you understand that?"

Nodding slowly, Gina smiled.
"I understand"

Liz began counting backwards. After she reached the number seventy five, she stopped and let Gina continue. As Gina counted, Liz spoke quietly.
"You're very tired. It's getting harder to focus on your counting. Just rest Gina, you're safe here, just rest."

A moment later, Gina's counting faded to nothing. Liz released the hold she had on Gina's hands.
"You're doing fine Gina. Can you hear me?"

The blonde head bobbed slowly. Liz smiled.
"I want you to think back Gina. We don't have to go far back in time. Why don't we go back just six months ago? Tell me what you are doing?"

Gina smiled. Her voice was soft and the words spoken slowly.
"I'm at my computer. I sell plaques I make. They have poems and sayings I engrave on the surface. Some also have illustrations. I just got an order for fifteen of my works. I'm so excited. It means a lot of work for me, but that's okay. They're custom orders, but I love making them."

Liz nodded. "Are you alone?"

Gina smiled. "I am now, my brothers just left."

Fascinated by the news she had just been given, Liz grinned.
"How many brothers do you have Gina? How old are they?"

Gina smiled broadly, her eyes remained closed.
"I have two brothers. One is two years older than me and one is just a year younger. He's nineteen."

Liz frowned. "What are their names?"

Gina shook her head and frowned.
"I can't remember. Isn't that strange? I should know my brother's names. What's wrong with me?"

Seeing Gina was getting upset, Liz spoke calmly.

"It's okay Gina. The names will come to you. Let's talk about something else. Do you know where you are at? Is the computer at your house?"

Gina nodded. "Yes, I have a nice little house. It just has two bedrooms, but that is enough for me. I turned one bedroom into my office and workroom."

Liz smiled. "That's fine Gina. It sounds like a wonderful home. Do you know the address at your house?"

Again, a frown line ran across Gina's forehead. "No, I can't think of the address. Damn it. No, wait, wait. I live on Eden Lane. You know, like the garden in the bible."
A large smile was followed by a quick laugh.
"I remembered, oh my gosh, I remembered."

Liz also laughed lightly.
"That's fantastic Gina. You're doing well. Can you think of the name of the town you live in or the state?"

Gina was quiet a moment. She started to shake her head, but then shrugged.
"I don't know the city, but I live in Washington State."

Nodding, Liz was amazed by what Gina could remember, although she wished the information was revealed at the same time, instead of in bits and

pieces. Liz tried to relax and not be impatient. Any results were a step in the right direction.
"Do your parents live in Washington as well?"

Gina frowned. "They do live in the state, but we live in different cities. Right now, I just can't think of either town."

Once again, Liz could see the frustration in Gina's face and hear frustration in her voice.
"I think we have looked back in time enough for one day Gina. You've done amazing. I'm going to count to ten. When I do, I want you to begin waking up. When I stop counting, I will once again take your hands and you will be awake. You will be able to remember all we talked about. Your mind, like you, is started to wake up. In time, your memories will all return. Do you understand all I've said?"
Liz waited for Gina to nod, before she slowly counted. Reaching the number ten, Liz reached out and took Gina's hands.

The light blue eyes opened slowly, and stared at Liz. The excitement in them was evident. Gina smiled. "I'm an artist. Can you believe it? And I have a family."
Gina frowned. "I just wish I could remember their names."

Liz nodded and gripped Gina's hands tighter.

"You'll remember. These things take time. In fact, you shared more than expected during this first session. Well done Gina."

The pride at what she accomplished was slightly shadowed by what she hadn't remembered, but all in all, Gina felt much better.
Liz stood, pulling Gina to her feet as well.
"Why don't we go out and check on Kelly? I'm sure she will like to know how well your session went. I know, like you, she has also been worried about being hypnotized."

Gina nodded. "I definitely was nervous. I'm just thrilled at how well it went."
Gina laughed. "I just wish everything could have been accomplished with one session."

Liz smiled. "That would have been nice. Things like this take time, but I have a good feeling we can resolve the problems you and Kelly are having."

The two women walked out to the living room, where Kelly was watching the news. Seeing them, Kelly grabbed the remote, and turned off the TV. Looking at the women, and their contented demeanor, Kelly felt her optimism rise.
"If I were to guess, I'd say things went well."

Both Liz and Gina nodded. Gina's blue eyes lit up. "I remembered quite a few things about my past. Liz is a miracle worker."

Rolling her eyes, Liz shook her head.

"I wouldn't go that far, but Gina's right, things did go well."

She frowned at Kelly.

"Are you ready for your session?"

A shrug was followed by Kelly, giving Liz a nod.

"I'm ready as I'll ever be. Seeing Kelly's face, I feel much better and hopeful for what might happen."

As Kelly stood, Gina took her place on the couch.

"I think I'll watch some television and see if anything else might trigger my memories."

Leaving Gina in the room, Liz and Kelly headed to Liz's office. Liz had Kelly sit in the chair that Gina had just vacated. She sat down across from her. Reaching out she took Kelly's hands in her own. She walked Kelly through what was going to happen. Restating what she had told Gina, when she had been in the chair. Using the same technique, Liz hypnotized Kelly, and began her questioning.

"Can you hear me okay Kelly?"

Across from her Kelly nodded. Liz spoke quietly.

"I want you to think back. Let's talk about your life just a few months ago Kelly. Can you tell me what you do on a typical day?"

Kelly nodded. "Sure. In the mornings I work part time at the daycare center. Two friends and I take care of children. They are all under five. Three of the kids go to kindergarten in the afternoons. We watch the children while their parents work. In the afternoons, I head over to my second job. I'm a part time receptionist at a law office."

Watching Kelly's face, even with her eyes closed, Liz could see the love for both of her jobs clearly evident.
"Can you tell me what town these jobs are in?"

Kelly nodded. "Sure, Carlton."

Surprised that Kelly had come up with the name, Liz then frowned.
"Do you know what state Carlton is in?"

A frown caused Kelly's mouth to droop. She shook her head. Her voice was aggravated.
"No, that's weird. No, I can't think of the state. What's wrong with me?"

Liz sighed. "That's okay Kelly. Don't worry about it. Nothing is wrong with you. I'm sure the name will come to you later. Now, what about your family? Do they live in Carlton?"

Kelly shrugged. "It's just mom and I. She lives here though. Our places are just a few blocks from each other. I'm lucky to have her so close."

Liz nodded. "Can your remember your address, or your mom's?"

Gently biting her lip, Kelly tried to think.
"My mom lives over on first street. I can't think of the street I live in. I just know its not far from my mom's place."

Liz nodded. "You're doing really good Kelly. We're really making great progress. What about the law office you work for, do you have a name for that place?"

Kelly laughed. "That's easy, Kline, Kline and Jones, attorneys at law. The Kline's are father and son. The Jones is actually the son's wife. All of them have been really good to me."
Staring at Kelly, Liz was surprised by how much information Kelly, like Gina had done, was able to recall.
"Can you remember your mom's name?"

Shaking her head, Kelly frowned.

Liz nodded. "That's okay. You're doing fine. Are you married Kelly?"

Kelly laughed. "That question is easy to answer. Nope, I'm single. I remember that because my mom is always asking me when I will get married and give her some grand-kids."

Liz laughed. "I can understand her feelings. I'd love some grandchildren running around myself. My son

hasn't decided to allow that yet, either."
Liz frowned. "Can you remember where you were
when you were abducted."

Frowning, Kelly shook her head.
"No, oh hell. I can see the road and those two
criminals who grabbed me, but I can't name the
place."
Kelly clenched her fists tightly and groaned.
"Why can't I remember that?"

Seeing Kelly was getting upset, Liz talked quietly.
"Never mind Kelly. Those memories will come back.
Right now, I'd say we've done more than enough for
our first session. I am going to bring you out of the
hypnosis, but when you wake, you will remember all
we talked about and the things you saw. Do you
understand me?"
Liz waited for Kelly to nod and then slowly brought
her out of the hypnotic trance.

Kelly, like Gina, was excited when she woke.
"That was amazing Liz. Thank you so much. I can't
remember everything, but at least I know my mom is
in Carlton, and will be looking for me."

Liz nodded. "I'll ask Frank to come by after work
and share the information both you, and Gina, came
up with. It doesn't seem like a lot, but with the tools
at the station at his disposable, Frank might find
answers we would never be able to."

Kelly smiled. Leaning forward, she gave Liz a hug. "Thank you so much Liz. What an astonishing thing you are doing. Without you, I don't know what, or where, Gina and I would be."

Returning the hug, then sitting back, Liz shrugged. "I'm just doing what feels right, and what I know how to do. I'm just glad for my training. I think the person who will be doing the most amazing things is going to be Frank. If you and Gina don't get many more memories back, I still feel Frank will find your families."

Kelly stared at Liz, then smiled.
"I hope so. Are we done for today?"

Liz nodded. "We are. I bet you and Liz will want to share your new memories. Let's go and see if she'd like a cup of cappuccino or a hot chocolate?"

As the two walked out of the room, Kelly frowned. "Is it summertime?"

Liz laughed. "Just about. It's the middle of June, tomorrow is flag day."

The light brown eyes lit up. Kelly was surprised she hadn't asked the date sooner. She guessed all else going on, was too overwhelming.

Liz let Kelly and Gina spend time talking about their sessions while she placed a call to Frank.

She didn't want to say much over the phone so she asked Frank to come for dinner again.
He readily agreed.

Several hours later, Liz, Kelly, Gina, and Frank, were in Liz's fenced backyard. The fence was six feet tall and lent a feeling of safety to all.
Liz had put Frank to work on the barbecue grill.

When she had first asked him to cook he had rolled his eyes.
"What, you want me to cook my own food? What kind of dinner invite is that?"

Liz laughed. "The best kind. Less work for me, Kelly, and Gina. Besides, the three of us aren't going to be just sitting around watching a handsome man cook for us. We have to fix the rest of the meal."

Frank's laughter blended with Liz's as he nodded. "Sounds like a plan to me, and a good one. I can't wait to hear about the day the three of you had."

Liz nodded. "It was interesting and informative. Just give the three of us a few minutes to put the other food together, while you cook the burgers and hotdogs. Then we can sit down and have a talk while we eat."

Nodding, Frank waved the large spatula, Liz had handed him, in the air. His dark eyes sparkled.
"I can't wait."

Within the hour, the food was done, and placed on plates. Four people sat at Liz's picnic table. Liz and Frank on one side, with Kelly and Gina on the other. They talked between bites of food. Kelly began first. "I remembered so much today. I feel like a new person."
The smile she wore, lit up her face.

Watching her, Frank liked what he saw. The fact that Kelly's smile, and her excitement were so genuine, touched his heart. He hoped in the days to come, he would be able to learn more about the woman, who had arrived in his life, in such a traumatic way.

Liz was nodding.
"Both Kelly and Gina had amazing sessions. I wrote all the information down for you to have. I'm hoping the additional information will help to find their families. We're still missing quite a few pieces of the puzzles, but we're gaining ground."

Nodding, Frank grinned.
"Great, I'll take that information. I won't be at the office tomorrow, but I will put the facts into the computer the day after."
Frank frowned and glanced around at the trio of women. Then he grinned.
"In fact, tomorrow I was thinking about taking a trip up to gather some wood. I'd be happy to have any, or all of you, join me."

Liz frowned and shook her head.
"You can count me out. I'm in no shape to be
running around the hills hauling wood."

Also shaking her head, Gina shrugged.
"I'll take a rain check on that. I'm a bit nervous to
even step outside. I don't mind being out here with
the tall fencing around the yard, but I'm scared of the
people from the institute finding me."

Nodding, Kelly stared at Frank.
"I agree with Gina. I'd love to go with you, though.
Do you think it's safe?"

A frown appeared as Frank shrugged.
"I don't know what those from the institute might try.
I'd say that you would be safe though. The places I
go to get wood, are what I'd call, 'off the beaten
path'. I can't guarantee anything for sure, but I
would promise you to do my best to protect anyone
that comes with me."

Kelly smiled. "That settles it then, I want to go."
She turned to Liz. "If it's okay with you. I know
you'll want to do another session tomorrow. Could it
wait until we get back?"

Nodding, Liz smiled. She thought Frank and Kelly
spending some time together would be a good thing.
"No problem, we can do the session when you get
back. I think getting out in the fresh air would do

you good."
Liz turned to Frank.
"I want you to promise me you won't work her too
hard."

Frank laughed and raised one hand.
"I give my word that I'll take it easy on her."

With a big smile, Liz nodded.
"That's settled then. I have one more surprise, if
everyone is finished with the dinner."

The others at the table, frowned and stared at Liz,
wondering what she was up to.

Standing, Liz looked around at the others.
"Everyone wait here. I need to grab my surprise
from the kitchen. I'll be right back."

As soon as Liz walked off, Frank, Kelly, and Gina
exchanged frowns, but no one spoke.
A few moments later, Liz came back carrying a cake.
"I called the bakery and ordered this. They delivered
it earlier. I had a hell of a time not letting Gina or
Kelly see it, especially Gina."

A large frown covered Gina's face. Her light blue
eyes darkened with curiosity.
"Why me?"

Placing the cake on the table, Liz laughed and pointed at the top of the cake where someone had written on it. Gina stared at the words.
"You're twenty now, congrats, Gina."

The blue eyes lit up. Gina clapped her hands.
"What a nice surprise. Thanks Liz."

Liz nodded. "You're welcome. After your session, when you said your age, I called the bakery, and ordered this cake. With all you and Kelly have been through, I thought this would be a happy sentiment. It's the little things that help take our minds away from the tragedies we deal with."

Rubbing his hands together, Frank was nodding. "The best part will be when you cut that cake, and I get a piece."

Liz's sapphire eyes sparkled.
"Alright then, cake for all."

Chapter 13

The next morning, although Kelly was up early, Liz was already in the kitchen. She turned as Kelly stepped in the room.

"Good morning. Grab some coffee. I made biscuits and gravy, if you're hungry."

Kelly smiled. "Good morning and thanks. You do so much for Gina and I. How will we ever repay you?"

Before Liz could answer, the two women heard the sound of Gina's voice, as she stood in the doorway.

"I don't think we can ever do that. Good morning to both of you."

She turned to look at Kelly who was pouring her coffee.

"Are you nervous about today?"

Kelly shrugged. "A little I guess. I know I can trust Frank, but I'm like you, going out into the world, even if it's in a remote spot, is unnerving."

It was Liz who spoke.

"Frank will take care of you. He's a wonderful person, and a hell of a policeman. I've known him for years. I don't have a bad word to say about that man."

Kelly smiled. "Good to know. I just hope I can do my share of the work. I laid in that bed at the institute for so long. I'm feeling good, but haven't gotten much exercise lately."

Kelly laughed. "I don't even know if I did much exercise before this whole thing started. I was abducted while jogging, but for all I know, I was a lazy person, who didn't do much."

Both Gina and Liz shook their heads at Kelly's assumption. Liz grinned at her.

"I'm sure that's not true. If it was, you wouldn't be in such good shape now. Are either of you going to have some breakfast with that coffee?"

Both women nodded and grabbed plates and served up breakfast. Kelly smiled.

"Thanks again Liz, I better eat so I have some energy for helping Frank."

A half an hour later, the sound of the doorbell could be heard. Liz stood.

"I'll answer that. I'm sure it's Frank, but you never know."

Sitting at the table, Kelly and Gina exchanged nervous glances. Both wondered what the chances were of someone coming to Liz's house that they should be afraid of. Seeing Frank, following Liz into the kitchen, the women relaxed, at least for the time being.

Frank shook his head at Liz's offer to have breakfast. "Thanks, but I ate at home. I'll have a cup of coffee though. Then, Kelly and I better get going."

Liz nodded. "When do you expect to be back?"

Franks shrugged. "We should be back shortly after lunchtime. Is that okay?"

Smiling, Liz nodded. "That's fine. Gina and I can do a session this morning, than Kelly and I can have one this afternoon."
She pointed at Frank.
"Just remember, you don't need to get wood for the whole town. Don't work Kelly too hard. She was just saying that she's been lying around and doing nothing for the last little while."

Frank laughed, his dark eyes filled with mischief. "We'll just fill up the back of my truck. I still have all summer to get more, if I need to."
Pushing back his chair, Frank stood and turned to look down at Kelly.
"I think we'd better get going."

Nodding, Kelly stood from the table.
"Do I need to bring anything?"
As she spoke, Kelly mentally shook her head, wondering what she would even be able to bring. At the moment she had no possessions.

She was glad when Frank shook his head.
"I have everything we'll need in the truck"
He waited for Kelly to stand before turning to look at Liz and Gina.

"We'll see you two later."

Both women said their good-byes, then watched
Frank and Kelly leave. Once they were gone, Gina
stared at Liz.
"Let me help you clean up in here."

Liz smiled. "Thanks. As soon as we're done, we can
go ahead and get started with your session."

While the two women stayed at the house, Kelly got
in Frank's truck. She could see a cooler and a
chainsaw sitting in the bed. Taking her seat on the
passenger side, Kelly slipped on her seat belt, before
turning to smile at Frank.
"Thanks for inviting me to come with you today."

Backing out of the driveway and then starting down
the rode, Frank nodded.
"Actually, I'm glad to have some company. I love
going out in the woods, but sometimes I get lonely
with just my own company."

It took about a half an hour before Frank brought the
truck to a stop. Kelly had spent the time staring out
the window. The woods they were in today, weren't
as thick as the ones behind the institute.

Turning off the truck, Frank pointed to a couple of
dead tress sitting on a small hill.
"Let's cut those down. After I use the chainsaw to
cut them in smaller pieces we can roll them down the

hill toward the truck."
Frank lifted the lid of the console that sat between him and Kelly. Reaching in, he pulled out two pair of gloves. He handed one pair to Kelly.
"I hope these aren't too big. You'll be glad to have them on for protection, even if they're a little large."

Nodding, Kelly took the gloves and smiled.
"Thanks Frank. I wouldn't have even thought about needing gloves."
She sighed and shook her head.
"For all I know, I've never gathered wood before."
A frown dug a groove in Kelly's forehead, as she worried if she would ever remember more about her past.

Getting out of the truck, Frank grabbed his chainsaw. The two walked up to the standing, but dead, trees. Kelly stood back while Frank first cut the tree so it dropped to the ground, then as he sawed the tree into smaller pieces.
She stepped over, and following Frank's example, rolled the cut logs. Walking from the area to the truck, Kelly grabbed a cut piece and carried to the truck bed. Throwing it in, Kelly could tell that by the time they were done, her arms were going to be sore. The two worked steadily until all the cut pieces had been stacked in the truck.

Frank wiped the perspiration from his forehead with his gloved hand. Turning to Kelly he smiled.

"You're a good worker. Do you feel up to loading up a couple more trees?"

Wiping her face, then nodding, Kelly smiled. "I'm okay. I don't know if I'll be able to say that tomorrow, but so far, I don't think you've worked me too hard."

The two got back in the truck and Frank drove further up the old, dirt road. After they had gone a short way, Frank pointed out the window. "There's a couple of trees we can get. That should just about fill up the back of the truck."

Kelly nodded, but frowned. "Who owns these woods anyway? Do they just let anyone come and get wood?"

Frank smiled at the questions. "Actually these woods are State property. As long as you pay for a permit, you can come and get wood. I like to get extra. So many people in town have wood burning stoves, and for one reason or another, can't come out here and do what we're doing today. I let them take whatever wood they need from the piles at my place."

Staring at Frank, Kelly was amazed by his generous spirit. "That's really nice of you. I hope they appreciate your hard work. I need to tell you thanks for what you did for Kelly and I as well. I don't know what we would have done if the two of us would have run into the sheriff before we met you. I'm positive he would have taken us right back to that institute."

Frank sighed. "I hate to say it, but you're right about Sheriff Bertram. Jim isn't the best caliber of person. I'm hoping to get enough information on his connection to the institute to have him fired. I also hope to get the institute shut down. After the episode the other night with a patient dying, that might be easier now than ever before. With Doctor Mengle given permission to bring death row inmates to the institute, he should be following Federal guidelines for their humane treatment. The sheriff will try to cover up what happened, but I'm going to do my damnedest to make sure he can't do that. I've already asked for an investigation."
Frank sighed and frowned.
"I hate to say it. But both you and Gina may be asked to testify if the investigation pans out."

Kelly frowned. "That scares me to death, but if it prevents another person from going through the horror that Gina and I did. I'll testify."

Staring at Kelly, Frank admired her courage. He knew both she and Gina were still trying to discover the past memories that had been stolen. He smiled. "You're a brave lady. I'm sorry for what you and Gina went through."

Kelly shrugged. "That death row inmate went through much worse. I'll be happy to do what I can."

Stopping the truck, Frank turned off the engine. "We better get busy on these trees, or I'll have to explain to Liz why I didn't get you back in plenty of time for your session."
Kelly laughed, thinking of Liz berating Frank. That was something she felt Liz could do, but she didn't think the woman ever would. It was easy to see that Liz loved Frank.

After the two loaded the trees, Frank grabbed the cooler out of the back of the truck.
"I packed water, pop, and a couple of sandwiches. How about we take a break before we head back to town?"

Nodding, Kelly smiled. "You really did think of everything. Thanks Frank. Thanks again for all you've done for me and for Gina."

Frank smiled seeing the genuine appreciation in Kelly's light brown eyes. He shook his head. "I didn't do much. Liz is the miracle worker. She does so much for so many."

Nodding, Kelly had to agree.
"Yes, Liz is amazing, but you deserve a lot of credit for all you do. I just hope that some day that Pine View Institute will be shut down permanently."

A shrug was followed by a slight grin.
"I have a feeling that now something will be done. Even the corrupt government isn't going to allow word to get out that death row inmates are being tortured and killed. Not to mention innocent people like you and Gina. There is one thing you should know, Gina as well."
Seeing the frown Kelly was giving him, Frank sighed.
"I've been working with an FBI agent. His name is Manuel Ortega. Manny is heading up the team investigating the institute. I have a feeling he will want to talk to you and Gina, maybe even Liz, to get what information he can on that place, the doctors and the nurses. You can trust him."

Shaking her head, Kelly let out a resigned sigh.
"I hate to talk to anyone, but Liz, about what happened, but if it will save others from going through the atrocities Gina and I did, then I'll talk to him."

Nodding, Frank started putting things back in the cooler. "Good to hear. I think it's time for you and I to head back. I don't want Liz yelling at me for having you out too long."

Thinking that Liz would never rebuke Frank for anything, Kelly laughed. Frank loved the sound. The brown eyes lit up.
"You're not scared of Liz are you?"

Frank shrugged, but laughed.
"Maybe a little bit."

The two gathered everything and put the things in
the back of Frank's truck, then they took their places
in the front. Driving back down the road, was a bit
different than traveling in had been.
To Kelly, every bump in the road was magnified.
Seeing the nervousness in her face as he hit one
bump, then another, Frank shook his head.
"Sorry about that. The extra weight of the wood is
playing havoc with the shocks. Don't worry, I'll get
you back safe and sound."

Nodding, Kelly believed the reassuring words, but
still was holding her breath with each bump and
bounce. When Frank hit an extra large hole, Kelly's
hands dropped to either side of her on the seat, trying
to steady herself. Glancing over, Frank felt awful, He
reached over and placed his hand on Kelly's.
"Everything is going to be okay."

The feel of Frank's hand on her own was comforting.
When he lifted his hand, to grab the steering wheel
with both hands, Kelly's spirit sank. There was
something about the contact she desperately needed.
That thought had her wondering if the trauma of the
happenings at the institute would ever fade. She had
a feeling that stress would be with her long into her
future, if not forever. That thought only made her
anger, and her resolve to not let the atrocities
continue, stronger.

Finally Kelly nodded at Frank's words.
"I trust you Frank."

Kelly's words brought a smile to Frank's face.
Knowing she felt trust in him, made Frank happy,
and hoping to get to know Kelly better.

When Frank turned on to the paved road, Kelly
breathed out a sigh of relief. Then she frowned.
"Do you want me to help you unload your truck?
You have a lot of wood on here."

Frank shook his head. "I'll do it. Believe me, I've
done that on my own, more times than I can count. I
want to get you delivered back to Liz's place."

A half hour later, Frank pulled the truck into Liz's
driveway. He looked over at Kelly.
"I'll walk you in."

The front door to the house opened before Kelly and
Frank had reached it. Liz was standing in the
doorway. She looked at Kelly, her gaze going from
the woman's head to her feet, before she turned to
Frank and gave him a smile.
"She doesn't look too worse for wear."

Frank laughed. "Nope, she's here safe and sound,
like I promised."

Liz laughed. "I didn't expect anything less. Come on

in for a minute. Gina and I just finished her session. Things went well, I think."

Kelly and Frank followed Liz into the kitchen, where Gina was seated at the table. The three joined her. Liz looked across the table at Kelly.
"Did you enjoy your working trip?"

Kelly nodded and smiled.
"I have to admit, Frank worked a lot harder than me, but yeah, it was fun."
Then she shrugged. "Well, maybe not the ride back so much. It was a bit rocky."
Kelly turned to look at Frank.
Watching the two, Liz was thrilled to see a special look pass between the two. She wasn't a matchmaker, but always loved to see a couple who seemed to have a special link.

Frank was nodding. "It's always that way when you have a heavy load."
Frank sighed. "Speaking of that, I really need to get going if I'm going to get my truck emptied out before dark."

Liz nodded. "I think Kelly could use a nice, hot bath. Then she and I have a session to work on."
Liz frowned. "I have to work tomorrow. When I get the information together on Gina and Kelly's sessions compiled, I'll come by the station before work and drop it off to you."

Frank nodded. "Sounds good."
He stood up and looked down on Kelly.
"Thanks for the help today. It was nice to have company. I don't get that often."
He turned to Gina and Liz.
"I'll talk to you both when I have more time."

After Frank left, Gina turned to Kelly, her light blue eyes shining.
"I had a couple of breakthroughs in my session today. I remembered my brothers' names. Aaron is younger than me and Garth is older. I even know where they live. It's like a miracle."
Gina shrugged. "Well, I can't recall their actual street addresses but I know the towns and even the states they live in."

Staring at Gina with wide open eyes, Kelly smiled. "That's great news. I hope I learn something that impressive in my session."

Liz nodded, then frowned.
"First, off with you to the tub. You can not only get cleaned up, but before too long, I bet you will be having some sore muscles from your work today. A nice hot soak in the tub might help with that."

All three women at the table nodded and laughed at what Liz had said. The sound was like music to all ears.

An hour later, Kelly sat across from Liz in her office. Liz had talked Kelly into the same hypnotic state she had the day before. With Kelly under hypnosis, Liz spoke quietly to her.

"Today, I'd like you to think back to a special memory. It doesn't matter if it was months, or years ago. I'd just like you to share a happy occasion."

Eyes closed, Kelly let her mind head back. A moment or two later, she smiled.

"It's my birthday. I just turned thirty two."
 The smile grew larger.

Liz was nodding. "Do you know what day it is."

A frown was followed by a nod.

"It's September. The eighteenth of September. My mom is here. She brought me a new pair of shoes for my birthday. I told her a few months ago that I was thinking about taking up jogging."

The sound of Kelly's voice was light and happy.

"My mom is so wonderful. She always remembers things like that. She always tries to pick presents that mean something special to the receiver."

Liz nodded. "Your mom sounds wonderful Kelly. Can you tell me her name?"

It took a moment for Kelly to reply, but when she did, she was smiling.

"Cindy, my mom's name is Cindy Mitchell."

Liz smiled. "That's great Kelly. Is there anything else you'd like to share?"

A deep frown line covered Kelly's forehead. She was having a hard time breathing as a frightening memory came to mind.
"I was wearing those shoes, jogging, when those guys grabbed me."
Kelly's hands went up to cover her mouth, her eyes remained closed. She shook her head back and forth vehemently. The hands moved to run through her short hair. She gripped the dark strands tightly.
"Oh hell, why? I don't understand, what's happening?"

Reaching out, Liz grabbed Kelly's hands and gently extricated them from her hair.
"It's okay Kelly. Those men are gone now. They can no longer hurt you. You're fine and safe. Listen to me Kelly. I'm going to count to ten, and you are going to wake up. The bad memories will be in your mind, but they won't frighten you anymore. The good thoughts will remain and override the bad. Do you understand?"

Kelly nodded, as Liz began counting.
When her eyes opened, she stared wide eyed at Liz. She wasn't thinking about the men who kidnapped her. Kelly's mind was focused on the recollection she had of her mom's face and name. She was grateful to Liz for that. Her voice was full of excitement.

"My mom is Cindy. Can you believe that? She looks like me."

Letting out a relieved sigh, Liz could tell her prompt for Kelly to remember the good, and not the evil, had worked.
"That is wonderful Kelly. I bet Frank can do a lot with that information."

Kelly nodded. "I think you're right. I'm beginning to think Frank can do anything."

Liz smiled at the statement. She also knew now that her earlier thoughts that Kelly and Frank had made a special connection, was a concrete one. She hoped when Kelly found where she had lived, and what her life was actually like, she'd still be open to keeping Frank in her world.

The two women, with the session now over, headed out to share the news Kelly had learned with Gina. The excitement in the house, had Liz thinking the three of them should celebrate with having a pizza or two delivered.

Chapter 14

The next morning, Liz left Kelly and Gina alone at the house. She would have liked to stay with the women, but had so many others who needed her help. She left early enough so she could stop at the police station, before heading to work.
Stepping in, Liz smiled at Frank, sitting behind the main desk.
"Are you the secretary today?"

Frank shrugged. "I'm alone here. Hopefully nothing happens today. I'd have to call Marna or close shop up, before going on a call."
Frank sighed. "Marna doesn't like to be bothered on her day off, and I can't blame her."

Liz frowned. "Where's Sheriff sell-out?"

Chuckling at the name, Frank stared at Liz. She could see a twinkle in his dark eyes.
"I have news you might enjoy hearing. Jim was called over to Fulton this morning. The agent in charge of investigating Pine View Institute was eager to talk with the Sheriff."

Liz smiled broadly. "Damn, that is good news. I wasn't aware of the investigation. To tell you the truth, I hope Bertram loses his job."

A sigh was followed by the shaking of Frank's head.

"That would make me the interim sheriff. I'm not sure I'm ready for that."
Blue eyes narrowed as Liz stared at Frank.
"Personally, I think you're more than ready. It would just be for a few months anyway. There's an election in the fall."

Frank laughed. "Yeah, and Jim's name is the top one on the list of those running."

Liz smiled. "They might have to get a big marker and block out his name. That is, if all goes the way I hope it will."
Liz held up a couple of pieces of paper.
"I wrote down the new information from the sessions I held with Gina and Kelly. I think this info will be enough to find their families."
Liz frowned. "Will those two be able to go home when you contact their families? Aren't they both a part of this investigation you are talking about?"

Frank nodded.
"I've been talking to Manny Ortiz, he's in charge of the investigation. He'll need to talk to them both. I'm going to try and use this new information to contact their families. Maybe I can somewhat explain to them what has happened. I'm sure Kelly and Gina's families will be making a trip here. I just want them to know it would be better for the two women to stay with you until this is over."
Staring at Liz, Frank frowned.

"That's okay isn't it? I kind of volunteered not only your services, but your home."

Liz laughed. "I'm glad you did. The two of them are welcome to stay as long as they need to. I also kind of got the feeling yesterday that you wouldn't mind Kelly staying around for an extended period of time."

Frank couldn't stop the grin that covered his face. "I guess I wouldn't mind that. The little time I've been able to spend with her has made me intrigued about her."

Nodding, Liz smiled.
"Good to hear. Listen, I need to get headed out of here. Come by the house later and fill the ladies in. Hopefully by then, you'll have reached their families."

Frank nodded. "I'll be there."
He watched Liz walk out of the station before he laid out the papers she had brought to him, on the desk in front of him.
Two hours later, Frank was amazed by what he had been able to find. He had the phone number for Gina's parents as well as one for Kelly's mom. He was surprised to learn that Kelly came from a town just an hours drive from Westbend. He had never even given much thought that Kelly was from Montana, the same state they were in now. Gina lived in Ecksley, Washington. The place was just

over four hours away. Staring at the phone numbers he had written down, Frank called Gina's mother first.

The woman answered the phone quickly.
Her 'hello' was timid.
If she had caller ID, Frank knew she would see the call was from Westbend Police Station. He could imagine Gina's family staying close to the phone since she had disappeared. Probably scared to death about what news might come with a call, like the one he was making.
"Is this Mrs. Harris? Brenda Harris?"

Standing in her kitchen, Brenda grabbed a chair, needing to sit down, afraid of what was coming.
"Yes, this is Brenda. Have you found Gina? Is she okay?"

Frank nodded. "Gina has been found. She is alive and safe."

Frank could hear the sound of the woman's breath being released, followed by relieved crying.
"Oh thank God, where is she? Why hasn't she called us?"

Taking a deep breath, Frank tried to explain. He finally remembered to give the woman his name, and let her know he was a deputy. It took him over twenty minutes to even begin to tell the horrific tale. He knew he left out a lot of information. What he

was saying though, had to be unbelievable. He also knew just knowing her child was alive, was the most important thing he could tell Brenda Harris. He gave Brenda the number of a hotel in town before he finally hung up. He was encouraged by how well the talk had gone with Gina's mother.
Punching in the number he had found for Kelly's mother, he wasn't surprised that the woman, like Brenda Harris had done, answered quickly.
"Hello."

Frank stared at the information on his desk as he answered back. This time he gave his name and credentials first.
"Hello, this is Frank Whitley. I'm a deputy at the Westbend Police Station. Do you have a daughter, Kelly Mitchell?"

In her house, Cindy was nodding.
"Yes, Kelly's missing. Have you found her? Is she okay?"

Frank nodded. "Yes, Kelly is alive and doing okay. In fact, she is here in Westbend, that's just about an hour away from Carlton. I know you'll want to see your daughter. Right now, Kelly is part of an investigation related to her abduction. She is in a safe house. I can't give you the number there. I can have Kelly call you later or you can come here. We have two hotels in town."

Cindy couldn't believe what she was hearing. After this long, everyone had told her the chances of Kelly being found alive, were extremely thin. She was trying to catch her breath. Finally, she felt calm enough to be able to speak.

"I'll be heading to Westbend. Can you give me the number of either of those hotels? As soon as I can make reservations, and gas up my car, I'll be driving over."

Frank smiled. "I'll give you the number. I want you to promise me you'll be careful and drive the speed limit. I know you're anxious to see your daughter. Let's make sure you get here safe and sound."

Cindy nodded. "I promise."

After Frank gave Cindy the number, he hung up the phone. Sitting at the desk, Frank couldn't remember a time when he felt more at peace. To be able to tell Gina and Kelly's families that the women were safe was like a miracle. He knew happy endings were hard to find in cases like these.

He was still on duty, when a woman who looked to be in her late fifties, walked in the door. It only took Frank one glance at the lady to know, she had to be Kelly's mother. Frank smiled broadly.

"I bet you're Cindy Mitchell. Your daughter looks a lot like you."

Smiling back, Cindy nodded.

"And you have to be Deputy Whitley. I recognize your voice."

Frank nodded. "Come in, and have a chair."
He looked at his watch.
"My replacement should be here in about fifteen minutes. I can try and give you a bit more information while we wait. After Marna shows up, you can follow me over to the safe house. I know a woman who will be ecstatic to see you."

Sitting down, Cindy listened as Frank filled her in on what he hadn't told her earlier on the phone. She couldn't stop shaking her head at the incredible and dreadful story. Her heart ached with a pain that she knew would take a long time to heal, if it ever did. One thing she knew for certain, her daughter's pain was worse. Cindy felt like crying. Instead she straightened in her chair, pushed back her shoulders, and gave Frank a smile.
"We can get through this. Kelly is such a strong person and I will be here for her, no matter what she needs."

Frank nodded, amazed by the woman sitting in front of him. He knew that Kelly shared her mother's strengths.
"I'm glad to hear you feel that way. Kelly's recovery will only go better with you in her corner."

As Frank spoke, Marna walked in the office.

Her red hair was pulled back in a sensible ponytail.
The green eyes narrowed, as Marna stared at the
woman sitting across from Frank.
"Time for me to go to work. I'm guessing you have
some things to share with me."

Frank nodded. "Marna, this is Cindy Mitchell. She's
Kelly's mother. She's staying at a motel in town. I'm
going to take her over to see her daughter."

The green eyes lit up.
"Hi Cindy. You must be so relieved to know your
daughter is okay."

Cindy nodded. "I feel like a huge weight has been
taken off my shoulders. Until I can see Kelly and
give her a big hug, I won't feel whole."

Marna nodded at that, and turned back to Frank with
a frown.
"Where's the sheriff? Why didn't he cover for you?"

A sigh was followed by a sideways grin.
"Jim probably won't be back today. He may be
absent even longer than that. He was called over to
Fulton to be interrogated by the people investigating
Pine View Institute."

A smile turned into a laugh, as Marna clapped her
hands together.

"That's the best news I've heard in a long time."
She looked at Frank before turning to glance at
Cindy.
"Why don't the two of you get out of here then?"

Frank stood. "Consider that done."
Motioning to Cindy, Frank had her follow him out of
the station. Once outside, he told Cindy to follow
him, and the two headed for Liz's house.

Frank and Cindy walked up to the house, where
Frank rang the bell.
Liz answered the door with a frown on her face. It
dissipated when she got one look at the woman with
Frank. Then she smiled.
"You must be Kelly's mother. The two of you look a
lot alike, despite the hair color."

Cindy smiled. "I've heard we look similar, a lot. You
must be Liz. Thank you so much for helping Kelly."

Liz shook her head. "Kelly, and Gina as well, are the
ones doing all the work. Come on inside. I'm sure
you're anxious to see her."

Nodding emphatically, Cindy, accompanied by
Frank, entered Liz's house. They followed Liz into
the kitchen where Kelly and Gina were standing.
Both women, cooking dinner, had their backs to the
doorway. Hearing the sound of people entering, they
both turned with curiosity in their eyes.

The sound of Kelly's screams of delight could be heard, followed by her yelling out.
"Mom, oh my gosh, how did you find me?"

Cindy pointed at Frank.
"This is the man to thank."
That said, Cindy ran forward, and pulled her daughter into a hug.

As the two embraced, Frank stepped over to Gina.
"Your parents are on their way. They had farther to drive than Kelly's mom. I expect them later tonight."

Hearing the news, Gina felt her legs go weak. Moving to the table, she pulled out a chair and dropped down into it. She didn't know whether to laugh or cry. After several moments, she was able to pull herself together. She stared up at Frank.
"Thank you so much."
Covering her face with her hands, Gina closed her eyes and shook her head. The last months had been such a nightmare and now she felt like her wildest dreams of happiness might come true.

Liz had a big smile on her face.
"Everyone sit down. I think we all have a lot to talk about. Gina and Kelly were making dinner. Let me get some more food ready, and we can all have dinner together. Nothing like good food, shared with good friends, to heal the wounds."

Liz didn't wait for confirmation of her request as she headed to the refrigerator to see what she could conjure up for all to eat.

A short time later, Liz placed several plates of food on the table. She brought out a large container of lemonade. Placing it on the table, she rubbed her hands together.
"I think we have everything we need. I wondered if anyone would mind my saying Grace? I think we all have so much to be thankful for right now."
With no objections, Liz remained standing, as she said the blessing, and then sat down to join the others.

While the five people at the table ate the dinner, they talked. Both Gina and Kelly shared with Cindy a bit of what happened at the institute. They also spoke of their escape. Kelly and Gina also gave thanks to Frank and to Liz for their incredible help.
Kelly frowned at her mom.
"I'll be staying here a bit longer. Frank says I will probably have to give testimony. I'd love to head home right now, but if I can stay, and make sure that institute is shut down, and shuttered up, I want to do that."

Cindy nodded. "I wouldn't expect you to do anything less than that. From what Frank told me, you still have healing to do. Healing, that Liz is the best suited to help you do. I plan on staying a few days. Once I am positive you are going to be okay,

I'll head back."

Cindy's hand went to her chest.

"I'm just so glad you're alive. People kept telling me that too much time had passed since you went missing, and to expect the worst. Thank God they were wrong."

Reaching over, Kelly took her mothers had and gripped it tightly.

"I love you mom. I'm sorry for the worry you endured. I've done a lot of recovery already. Liz is a miracle worker."

Kelly looked across the table at Frank. Everyone in the room could see the admiration and warmth in her blue eyes.

"Frank has been a great strength for both Gina, and I. The two of us were lucky to step into Westbend Police Station and find him behind that desk."

Cindy's eyes narrowed for a brief moment before she nodded and smiled. She had noticed the look her daughter had given Frank. Cindy wondered if that was because she was grateful the man had saved her, or if more was going on. Cindy couldn't remember Kelly ever getting into a serious relationship. She had no problem with Frank being the first to have Kelly contemplating having one now.

Frank left the house after dinner, and a few hours of talking. He wanted to check out the hotels to see if Gina's parents had arrived.

Cindy remained visiting with Kelly and the other's at
Liz's house. Now that she had Kelly in her sights,
she feared leaving her daughter.
Although she knew Kelly was thirty two, and able to
take care of herself, Cindy's mothering instinct had
kicked in big time.

An hour later, the four women at the table exchanged
excited looks, when the doorbell sounded.
Liz stood and looked at Gina.
"That might be your folks. Better let me answer the
door, in case it isn't."
Gina nodded, but felt her emotions riding high. Hope,
that it was her mom and dad, coupled with the fear,
someone from the institute might have found her and
Kelly's safe haven.

A few minutes later, Liz came back followed by
Frank and a man and a woman. Gina jumped up
from the table and ran over to the couple.
She embraced both in extended hugs, before turning
to the others in the room.
"I'd like all of you to meet my parents. Seth and
Brenda Harris."
Introductions were made before the whole group sat
down at the table.

Liz stood to pull chips, pretzels and crackers, from
the cupboard before grabbing more lemonade.
Kelly and her mom helped grab plates, and cups,
before all were once again seated.

Once again, stories were told of Gina and Kelly's ordeal, and where things were expected to head. The Harris', like Cindy Mitchell, said they would also spend a few nights in town.
Brenda turned to Gina.
"We expect your brothers to arrive tomorrow. They both are eager to see you."

Gina smiled and nodded.
 "I can't wait to see them. Like Kelly, I plan on staying here to help with the investigation. Another atrocity, like the incident at Pine View, should never be allowed to happen. Hopefully, Kelly and I can prevent anything like that."

Everyone nodded, but Frank was thinking of how many times a government fronted experiment had caused horrific things to happen. Usually, once the public learned of the atrocities, the places were closed down. He knew in a lot of cases, the same places were reopened. Just in a new area, until they were caught again. He didn't say what was on his mind. He didn't want to damper the hopes and good spirits in the room.

Liz had similar thoughts in her mind. She felt she could help to bring normalcy to Kelly and Gina's lives, but felt that the government would do something similar to what Frank was also thinking.

For now, the two stayed silent and let the happy reunions continue.

Chapter 15

Three days later, Kelly and Gina's families were still in town. The two women had been brought clothes and new cell phones by their families. Both women had given their promises to keep in close touch once their families left town.
The two had stared in wonder at the new phones, both wondering where their old ones were at. The phones had gone missing when the women had each been abducted. Stolen, like so much of their past, had also been robbed from them.

Kelly and Gina had just finished sessions with Liz. Now, they were seated at the kitchen table, once again with their families, waiting for Frank. He had called Liz, to say he had news on the sheriff, and asked if Gina and Kelly were up to a visit from Manuel Ortiz. Knowing the two could deal with any questions, Liz still had asked for, and gotten, permission from the two, for the meeting.

When the doorbell rang, Gina and Kelly both felt their hearts skip a beat. Knowing what they were going through, Liz had smiled.
"Don't worry. Everything will work out fine. Frank and I will stay in the room while you talk with Mister Ortiz. I know you'll want your family members here as well. Remember, Manuel's on your side in all of this. If all goes well, it will be his team that shuts that damn place down. Hopefully that will

also be when those who did this, face criminal charges.”

Knowing Liz was right, both nodded, but couldn’t quite steady their anxious nerves.

Frank came back with Liz. A man, in his forties, stood just behind Frank. He had short, almost black hair, and green eyes, that were in sharp contrast to the dark hair.
When he smiled toward Kelly and Gina, the two women could see the compassion and caring.
Their nervousness dropped down a notch.

Frank looked at Gina and Kelly, and smiled.
“I’d like you both to meet Manuel Ortiz. He’s the lead investigator looking into the institute. I trust Manuel and I know both of you, can place your trust in him as well.”

Stepping over, Manuel shook each woman’s hand, as Frank said their names. He smiled.
“You can call me Manny. I’m sorry for intruding, especially with all you have both been through. I’d just like to ask a few questions.”

Kelly and Gina nodded. Liz, who had been introduced to Manny, when she let him and Frank in the house, motioned to the table.
“Manny, why don’t you and Frank sit down? I hope you don’t mind, I told Gina and Kelly I would stay with them while you visited.”

Nodding, Manny smiled. "If you wouldn't have
stated that, I would have asked you to be here. I
know you've been helping these two women. I've
heard only good things about the work you do. I'm
glad to see the family members here also."

Looking at Manny, Liz shrugged.
"I do my best. My biggest hope would be that things
like this never happened, and my services weren't
needed."

Sitting down, Manny nodded, but sighed.
"That would be my wish as well."

He stared at Gina and Kelly.
"I'd like to hear your stories. If the two of you could
start with what you can remember from the time
when you were abducted, until your escape, I'm
eager to listen."

Kelly and Gina exchanged concerned looks.
Kelly sighed. "You were taken first, but if you want,
I could talk first."

Gina shrugged. "I'm okay to tell what I can first."
Drawing in a deep breath Gina started speaking.
She didn't stop for an hour.
Manny listened and tried not to interrupt. He knew
how hard reliving the horror had to be.
When Gina stopped taking, Kelly began.

Like Gina, Kelly spoke for close to an hour, then both women spoke. They took turns speaking about the times they had been together. Trying to explain the atrocities they suffered, during the experiments Doctor Mengle had done. Although they knew their experience was hard for the family members to listen to, it was also a part of healing for all.

When both women finally fell silent, Manny nodded. "Thanks to both of you for sharing what happened. I know this was a traumatic experience. I hope the two of you telling your stories, will help prevent things like that from happening to anyone else. I'm so sorry for what you have gone through."
Manny turned to Frank, a slight smile on his face.
"I think Frank has some news he'd like to share before I explain to you what my investigative team is doing."

Frank nodded. "Thanks Manny."
He glanced around the table at all three woman before continuing.
"I have some good news, and some bad. I'll tell you the good first, because I have a feeling the bad is really just in my head."
Frank laughed at the curious looks he was given.
"The good news is, Sheriff Bertram will not be returning to the station. He isn't in jail, but is on home confinement while the investigation goes on. It seems that Jim received several large deposits in his bank account. All came from the Pine View Institute. Payments he had no business receiving. I think Jim

Bertram is still trying to come up with a plausible explanation for the payments."

Liz smiled. "That is good news, but what's the bad?"

Frank shrugged. "With Jim no longer in charge, I've been appointed the interim sheriff."

Liz stared at Frank, her eyes dancing.
"That sounds like good news, and better news, to me. No bad news in that whole conversation."

Both Gina and Kelly were nodding. Kelly lifted her hand and gave Frank a thumbs up.
"You're the best man for the job. Congratulations."

A bit embarrassed, Frank lifted his shoulders slightly in a small shrug.
"Thanks. I guess. I'm a bit nervous to take over, but I'm sure everything will work out. One thing I know is I'll have to hire a deputy. Marna and I will be needing the extra help."

Manny was nodding.
"Now, that brings us back around to the investigation. My team has been talking to a judge. We are trying to get a court order to allow us into the institute. We want to have a good look around. Hopefully before anyone destroys evidence. I know my team doing the investigating, might sound easy, but with the government backing the projects up there, it is a tricky situation all around."

With a sigh, Manny shrugged.
"I have a feeling the judge will put out the order. The fact that a prisoner died, as well as a worker, means things aren't looking so hot for Pine View, or Doctor Mengle and the others, right now. I'm hoping the judge will put out that order without sworn testimony from either Kelly or Gina."

Kelly frowned, staring at Manny.
"I'll be more than happy to give my testimony if it's needed. That place need to be shuttered up for good. That doctor, and the other one up there, along with all the workers, should be held accountable."

Gina nodded. "I'm with Kelly. Doctor Mengle was the one who hypnotized Kelly and I. but Doctor Anders went along with everything. The nurses never tried stopping anything either."

Staring at the women, Manny was nodding.
"I appreciate you both stating you are willing to help. Let me see how things go first. I'll keep in touch, either directly with the two of you, or through Frank."
Manny stood.
"I think I've taken up enough of your time for tonight. Thanks again for the help."

Frank stood. "I'll walk you to the door."

As the two men left the room, Cindy Mitchell stared at her daughter in dismay. Seth and Brenda Harris held the same looks as they stared at Gina.
Cindy spoke, saying when all three were thinking.
"I'm so sorry this happened. It's unbelievable to even think something like this could happen in this country and in this day and age."

A sigh sounded as Liz shook her head.
"Things like this have been going on for decades. The saddest thing is, even if that institute is shut down, there are many more like it, in other hidden locations."

The group around the table, began talking about other secret projects they had heard about.
Frank joined in when he re-entered the room.
When Gina yawned, followed by the same from Kelly, their family members stood.
Seth was the one to speak.
"I think Gina and Kelly have had enough excitement for one day. Time for them to get to sleep."
He smiled at Gina, but turned to Liz.
"Would it be okay if Brenda and I return tomorrow? We'd like to bring our two sons, if that's okay?"

Smiling, Liz nodded. "You'll always be as welcome here as Gina is."
She turned to Cindy. "The same goes for you. I'm sure you'll want to all spend as much time together as you can."

Cindy smiled. "Thanks for that, and thanks for taking care of Kelly and Gina. The two of them are so lucky to have you helping them. If you ever need anything, just ask."

Liz smiled, before she also stood.
"I'll walk you out. I've told Gina and Kelly to stay away from the doors. I'm still worried that somehow, people from the institute, could find this hiding place."

When Liz came back, Frank was standing at the table saying his own good-byes.
"I have to work tomorrow, but will come by during my lunch break. Marna and I are going to be doing double duty until I get a new deputy lined up. I've had a couple of people who have filled in the last couple of years during vacations. I think either, or both, of them will come help."

Liz smiled, as she took a seat.
"Come by around noon or so, and we'll have lunch waiting for you. I don't have any appointments until late afternoon."

Frank smiled. "Thanks Liz, I'll be here and I'll bring my appetite with me."

Not long after all the company left, Liz, Gina and Kelly headed for the beds. After the long day, they were tired enough to actually get a good night's sleep.

In the morning, Liz told Gina and Kelly their
sessions could wait until evening, or if they were
busy, they could even skip a day. She wanted to put
together plates of appetizers, knowing company
would be arriving. She figured that was the easiest
way to have food available, no matter who stopped
by, or at what hours.
Glad for a way to fill up time, Kelly and Gina were
happy to help.

At noon, Frank stopped by. When he sat down at the
table to eat, he smiled at the others. He started
talking before he began eating.
"Manny called. The judge he was talking about last
night, issued the order to allow Manny and his team
access to the institute."

Kelly frowned. "Then what happens?"

Frank shrugged. "Then we will probably have a bit
of a waiting game. It all depends on what they will
be able to find. Manny said some of the patients have
already been moved to different hospitals in the area,
while the investigation is on going. My guess is that
Manny, and his team, will have their schedule
packed between searching the institute and
interrogating those who work there, and then talking
to the patients, to see what they can remember."

Gina shook her head.
"Unless they have a miracle worker, like Liz, on

their side, that might not amount to much."
Then she frowned. "What about the patients who were brought to the institute from death row? Will they go back to jail?"

Frank nodded. "After they are treated at the hospital, yes, they'll have to. From what I can figure out, there were only seven inmates. Now, one of them is dead. It shouldn't take long to find prisons to take the others in."

With a deep frown, Kelly sighed.
"That's so sad. I'm sure they were excited to volunteer, just for that chance to get off death row. They had no idea what they were getting into. Now, one man is dead, and the other prisoners will be dealing with whatever mind games were played, trying to find answers to it all."

Liz sighed. "It's terrible what atrocities one human can do to another."

Trying to change the subject, Frank turned to look at Kelly and Gina.
"What time are you expecting your families?"

Both woman shrugged, Gina answered.
"I hope soon. I feel like it's been a decade since I saw my brothers. I can remember their faces, but not much more about them. I hope seeing them will bring some of my memories back."

Kelly sighed. "I just have my mom. I suppose she'll be here soon. I could have called her. She brought me a new phone. It's funny, after all this time without my cell phone, I never even thought of doing that."

Liz laughed. "That is strange, Usually old habits die hard. I check my phone several times a day, even when I'm not expecting calls, or have the need to call someone."

Nodding, Kelly shrugged. "To tell you the truth, I can't remember if I used mine a lot or not. It's kind of nice not to worry about calling, or even getting on the internet, to see what is happening in the world. I just feel at peace."

Frank smiled. "That's wonderful to hear. You and Gina went through more in a short time than most go through in a lifetime. You deserve to be at peace."

Staring at Frank, Kelly wondered how hard it was going to be to leave Westbend, and this interesting man behind, when the time came for her to return home. She had a feeling it would be one of the hardest things she had to do.

Chapter 16

A week later, both Kelly's mom, and Gina's families, had long since left Westbend.
Gina was packing up her few belongings, preparing to head home to Ecksley, Washington. She had decided her treatments with Liz had come to an end, and had decided she needed to get back to her life. Kelly wasn't ready to leave yet. She remembered having two jobs, but didn't feel the need to hurry back to either. She knew her job helping children was one she enjoyed, but because of the lapses in her memory, she didn't feel she should be working with children. Her other, part time job working in the law office didn't feel like something she wanted to do again.

Gina closed the small suitcase and turned to stare at Kelly. Tears stood in her light colored eyes.
"Promise me you'll call all the time. I want to know what you decide to do. No matter what you do, or where you go, I want to stay in contact. You are the one part of my life that stands out most to me. I feel like you and I have known each other forever."

Kelly nodded and held her arms out wide. As soon as Gina stepped into them, Kelly nodded.
"I'll keep in touch. I feel the same as you. I think the extraordinary circumstances of our time together has made us special friends and closer than family."

Stepping back, Gina wiped tears from her face. She turned to look at Liz, standing in the doorway.
"Thanks for all you've done Liz."
Shaking her head, Gina gave a light laugh.
"No words, can say how appreciative I am. You'll never know what a special lady you are in my eyes."

Stepping forward, Liz hugged Gina.
"It was my pleasure."
The sound of a doorbell had Liz stepping back and frowning. Gina's mom, who was picking her up, wasn't due for about an hour. Any unexpected company made Liz nervous. She knew the investigation into Pine View Institute was going well, and moving quickly, but she was still afraid of someone associated with that place finding the two women she considered family now.
She glanced quickly at Kelly and Gina.
"You two wait here. I'll go see who that is."

Kelly and Gina sat on the edge of Gina's bed and waited. Neither spoke, unsure of what to say.

A few minutes later, Liz came back smiling.
"We have a nice surprise this morning."
She motioned at the man in the hall.
"Don't just stand out there Frank. Let Kelly and Gina see your handsome face, so they know nothing is wrong."

Stepping in the doorway, Frank laughed and shrugged. He rubbed his chin.

"I don't know about handsome, maybe nice looking is a better description."
He looked over at Gina and Kelly.
"Sorry if I scared you. I know I should have called first, but I have a surprise for you both."
He turned to Liz.
"I think this is something you'd enjoy seeing as well."
As all three woman frowned at Frank, he smiled.
"If you would all indulge me with a bit of trust, I'd like all of you to take a ride with me. I borrowed Marna's SUV. I didn't want to use the patrol car, and my truck doesn't have much room."
Frank looked at Gina's packed suitcase.
"I called your mom. I hope you don't mind. I told her you would give her a call after we take this little ride."

All three women's faces were filled with curiosity. Gina shrugged. "I don't mind, but what is this all about?"

Shaking his head, Frank gave Gina a sly, sideways grin. "Oh no you don't. I'm not giving out any secret hints. Come on, let's get in the SUV."

The three women followed Frank from the house. Liz locked the door behind them. Frank asked Kelly to sit in front with him, and asked Gina to sit just behind Kelly. He got in behind the wheel, with Liz behind him. He smiled again as he looked around at the occupants of the SUV.

"I want Kelly and Gina to have the same view when
we get to the place I have in mind."

Kelly and Gina frowned, but didn't ask questions.
Instead they stared out the side windows, wondering
just where Frank was taking them. Behind Frank. Liz
was wondering the same. As he started driving, Liz
sat back in her seat. She knew the road Frank was
taking and had an idea where they were headed.
She also knew not to say anything about their
destination. She knew Frank would explain when the
time was right. Even though she knew where the
group may end up, she didn't know why yet.

Frank drove slowly. He wanted to arrive at just the
right time. Fifteen minutes later, he began driving
down a narrow road lined with pine trees.

Kelly and Gina stared out their windows. Just ahead
of them, on their side of the road, they could see
flashing lights. Several police cars were parked
haphazardly ahead. Frank pulled over about a half a
block from the scene.
Both Kelly and Gina could see a tall rock fence. Just
inside the fence line, a two story house made from
the same rock could be scene.
Staring at the place, Kelly frowned.
"Is that Pine View Institute?"

Looking over at her, Frank nodded.
"Actually, that house was once a summer retreat for
a couple. The place was sold when they passed away.

I'm sure they would hate seeing what the place was turned into. The house itself is not a part of the institute. It's more of a facade to keep the place hidden from prying eyes. The actual institute is in the building that was built just behind the house. You cant really see it from here and that's how the people behind the institute wanted it."

From the backseat, Gina pointed toward the police vehicles. "What's going on up there?"

Frank chuckled. "That is the surprise I brought you here to see. Just keep watching."
Frank turned so he could see Liz behind him.
"That goes for you as well. I think you'll find this interesting and well deserved."

Liz frowned, but turned so she could see out of the SUV's windshield. No one had to wait long. A few minutes after they had pulled in, and started watching, several people came out of the building. The group recognized Manny, who was tugging on the arm of a man whose hands were handcuffed behind him.

Recognizing the man, Kelly turned to Frank, eyes sparkling with excitement.
"Oh my gosh, he did it, Manny did it. That's Doctor Mengle that Manny is pulling with him."

Behind Kelly, Gina was nodding.

"It is him, I'd know that awful person anywhere."
Gina pointed.
"Look, that's Nurse Adams as well."

In the backseat, Liz was staring. She had never seen anyone that had worked at the institute. With the work she had done with Kelly, Gina and Frank, she felt like she not only knew them, but also knew the dark hearts, those people from the institute had, as well.

Turning from the scene outside, to Frank, then to Gina and Liz, before looking back at Frank, Kelly was almost afraid to ask the question on her mind. She drew in a deep breath.
"Is it over? Is the nightmare really over?"

Frank nodded. "Oh, there will be a trial and probably several appeals, but the doctors, nurses, and many of the workers, will sit in a jail cell through it all. Manny has an iron tight case showing the atrocities done in this place."

Gina was frowning.
"Where are the patients?"

Frank smiled. "They are safe. Manny moved them all. Last night he picked up Doctor Anders and the people working the night shift. When he told me he was arresting Mengle and the day workers today, I wanted to bring you all here."
Pulling out his phone, Frank called Gina's mother.

"Hi Brenda, it's Frank. We're all headed back to Liz's house now. We should be there in ten minutes."
He nodded at whatever the woman and said.
"Okay, see you there."

Hanging up the phone, Frank turned to Gina.
"I told your mom what was happening earlier."
He started the SUV, and then spoke out loud so all could hear.
"Looks like this show is over. Let me take you ladies home."
As he drove, Frank had a big smile on his face. He was happy to chauffeur the three women, whose enthusiasm and happiness for the ending of a dark chapter, was evident in their excited voices as they spoke over each other in their exuberance.

Later that evening, Liz and Kelly were alone in the house. The place felt empty. Liz was thinking how much worse it would feel when Kelly, too, was gone. So, Kelly's next words, although surprising, were also welcome.

Kelly was frowning.
"Liz, I've been meaning to talk to you about something. I'd like to ask you a favor. Before I do, I want you to know that if, for whatever reason, you want to say no, I'm okay with that."

Liz stared at Kelly, but didn't speak, waiting to hear what was on the woman's mind.

Kelly cleared her throat, then spoke quickly.
"I've been thinking how much I admire what you
can do. I did some research on that phone mom
brought me. I see you can take on-line classes in
psychology and other things like that. I'm thinking
about trying to help others who have problems like I
did. I have no idea about the hypnosis part, but I
think I could learn with a good teacher. Would you
consider teaching me? If you would, I also wonder if
you might be willing to take in a border? I don't feel
like there's anything left for me in Carlton. My mom
is there, but the town is just a few hours away. I'd
like to take a week and go back. I could visit with
my mom and tie up some loose ends, but after that. .
."
Kelly shrugged and smiled.
" . . . After that, anything is possible."

Liz laughed. "You said that so fast, I'm not sure I
caught it all. I think I got the gist of it though, and
the answer is yes, definitely yes."
Looking at Kelly, Liz gave her a knowing smile.
"All of your plans wouldn't also involve getting to
know the new sheriff in town would they?"

Smiling back, Kelly shrugged.
"Like I said, anything's possible."

<u>*Chapter 17*</u>

The lake appeared dark blue, in the chilly afternoon weather. Reflections of white clouds seemed to cause them to float, not only in the sky, but in the water.
Staring out at the lake, Kelly was thinking of all she and Gina had been through in the three months since their escape from Pine View Institute.

The two women, along with the other patients from the institute, had been give CT scans. Kelly had been so nervous about hers, she had thrown up in the facilities bathroom before the test had actually taken place. She couldn't stop thinking about the connection that had been placed on the back of her neck and then run to Gina's, in the same spot.
The results of the scan, luckily showed that Doctor Mengle had not implanted anything into the back of her neck. Gina and the other patients, had been given that same good news. All tests and treatments were being paid for by the government. They had also worked out payments to the patients, in the form a large settlements.

Kelly and Gina had given a large portion of their payments to Liz. They asked her to join them in creating a place for others who suffered mental and physical abuse. The hospice like house, had been built on the property next to Liz's home. The facility allowed people a place to stay while they recovered.

Kelly was learning how to complete that treatment. She wasn't a hypnotherapist, like Liz, but she had found she had some special talents when it came to working with patients.

After Kelly had learned that no implants had been placed in her neck or brain, she still worried about the things that Doctor Mengle had forced her and Gina to do. She was horrified to think that some residual effect would continue long after escaping from the madness of the institute.

Instead of creating evil, like Mengle, Kelly found she had a unique talent for healing. She was practicing holistic medicine. She was fond of the practice of acupressure. She discovered when she touched a patient, she felt a tingling in her fingers. At first, that had terrified her, then, when the patients' recoveries were sped up, she was overwhelmed with the talents she found inside of herself.

She still worried that one day, the evil would show itself and she would have to stop doing the new job she loved.

Kelly and Gina kept close contact. They talked and texted each other almost everyday.

When Kelly told Gina the discovery she had made, she could hear the sound of Gina's delighted squeal over her cell phone.

"Oh my gosh Kelly. I'm so happy you told me about what is happening with you. I noticed when I do my artwork, my fingers feel all tingly. The work I have produced lately is the best I have ever done. I just

feel a special connection between my hands and whatever project I am working on."
Nodding at her own words, but also frowning, Gina sighed.
"Do you think this is all because that creep, Mengle, ran the cable between us to do the experiments?"

Thinking about what Gina suggested, Kelly shrugged. "I don't know Gina. As long as the two of us are using whatever strange talents we received for good, I'm not going to question the how or why. I believe everyone has special talents, and if we enhance them, they will grow. Mengle may have activated them, but what either of us can do, is for good, not evil, like that man was doing."

Gina was frowning, holding the phone tightly. "What if that changes? What if you or I do something that puts someone else in harm's way?"

Thinking of Gina's beautiful artwork, and the good she had done for others in the last few months, Kelly shook her head.
"I don't think anything like that will happen. The evil comes from Doctor Mengle and the others at the institute. I'm positive that as long as you and I want to do good and make others happy, that is what will make the difference."

Feeling reassured by Kelly's words, Gina smiled. "You're right Kelly. I'm so glad that is how you think about all this. I feel the same. As long as we strive to do good and help others, things will work out. When you help someone, there at Safe Haven, my spirits soar. When I'm able to create beautiful artwork, that can make others' spirits rise, I feel good. Thanks so much Kelly, I feel so much better and have more confidence in what I am doing."

Hanging up the phone after that conversation, Kelly also felt better about what she was doing, and about life in general. She also wondered if the patients she had never even seen at the institute, were finding their own talents enhanced. Kelly could only hope they also used their gifts for doing good. Her main concern was those who had come to the institute from death row. Which way would they lean? Toward the light, or into darkness, like Mengle, and the others? Kelly tried to not focus on that aspect. She had her own life to get moving on with.

Thinking back to the week she had spent with her mom, before coming back to stay with Liz in Westbend, Kelly was glad she had decided to make the move. The first thing she had done when she got back to Carlton was to tell her landlord that she wouldn't need to rent the place anymore. Kelly had gone to the law office she had worked at part time, and told them she couldn't continue working there. After all the time she was gone, Kelly wasn't surprised to see another person sitting at the desk she had once occupied.

Going to the daycare center was the hardest part of
what Kelly had to do. Stepping in the building, and
seeing the faces of the children, had memories
flooding Kelly's mind. She felt like she was having a
sensory overload. Trying not to show her feelings,
Kelly had finally headed to the bathroom, locked the
door, and dropped to the floor.
Her hands had covered her face as tears rolled down
her cheeks. Kelly was overwhelmed. The happy
memories of the time spent at the daycare had
blended with the anger at all those involved with
Pine View Institute, and what they had done. Not
just to her, but to Gina and the other patients.
Sitting on the floor, in that bathroom, Kelly had let
the tears come. She felt like they were washing away
her anger and allowing her to leave Carlton. She
knew she could do much more for others in
Westbend. Her own revelations had also allowed her
to explain better to her mom why she needed to
leave.

The sound of Frank's excited voice beside her,
brought Kelly our of her reverie.
"Hey, you got a bite Kelly. Lift up your pole, then
reel it in."

Confused for a minute, as she stepped from
daydream to reality, Kelly finally nodded.
She jerked hard on the pole, then watched as the
hook, and the attached fishing line, flew up and out
of the water with no fish in sight.

Kelly laughed and shook her head. She turned to stare at Frank, humor shining in her eyes.
"Oh no, I'm sorry about that Frank. I guess I was startled and jerked too hard. I was lost in thought and forgot to focus on what I was doing."

Joining in the laughter, Frank shook his head.
"No need to be sorry. I don't know if we'll be having a fish fry for dinner though. Neither of us is having any luck."

With a grunt, Kelly shrugged.
"To tell you the truth, I don't even like fish."

A frown line covered Frank's forehead.
"Why didn't you tell me that before? We could have found something else to do today."

Kelly smiled. "This trip isn't about catching fish, Frank. I just am happy to be with you in this peaceful place. I think I needed some relaxing time. I'm a bit worried about heading to meet your family this weekend."

Frank stared at Kelly, his dark eyes opened wide.
"Really? You don't need to worry about that. My family is really excited to meet you. I have to tell you, the bunch of them are always telling me I need to be in a relationship. My parents have been married for over forty years. All my brothers and sisters are married as well."

Kelly's own eyes opened wide as she nodded.
"That's what I'm talking about. You having three
brothers, and two sisters. I'm an only child raised by
a single mom. I'm not used to a crowd like that. Not
even close."

Frank laughed. "You'll do fine, they're all going to
love you."

Kelly grunted. "I don't know about that."
Then she frowned again.
"Do any of your family look like I do?"

Although the two of them seldom talked about their
interracial relationship, Frank knew that was what
Kelly was talking about today. He shrugged.
"I have one brother married to a woman with red
hair. I also have a sister married to a woman with
blonde hair. I don't think you have to worry that
you'll stand out in the crowd."

Relieved, Kelly nodded. She watched Frank pull his
fishing pole out of the water. He put it on the ground
beside him, then stood. Walking toward the edge of
the water, Frank picked up a rock.
He turned back to Kelly and grinned.
"Instead of fishing, can you do this?"
Frank pulled the arm, holding the rock, backwards at
a side angle. He let the rock go.

Kelly watched the rock skip across the top of the
water three times, before finally dropping down into

the liquid depths. Smiling she stood up and found her own rock. Kelly took a moment to rub the rock back and forth in her hands. She turned to Frank, shrugged, then smiled broadly.
"Here goes."
She let the rock fly. She and Frank watched the rock skim the surface of the water. It dipped gently, then rose, eight times before it had finished its journey, by sliding gently into the water.

Frank stared at Kelly.
"Wow, I'm impressed. Seems to me, you're a lady with some hidden talents."

Kelly only smiled as Frank walked over to her, slid his arm around her waist, then bent down to kiss her. When Frank finally pulled back he smiled.
"I think that's the talent I like best of all."

Kelly laughed. "All that talent needs is a whole lot more practice."

Frank also laughed.
"That, we can do."
He leaned down to start practicing.

Thanks so much for reading this book. My readers
are so amazing and have such vivid imaginations.
You bring the words to life, and I thank you for that.

I am fascinated by the mind and what it is capable of.
So much is unknown. If we could tap into the power
of the mind, what could we accomplish?
My biggest hope is that we would use what we find
we can do, for good. Of course, evil is always
hanging around looking for ways to thrive.
That's why I try to write books where good wins, but
there's always the other possibility waiting in the
shadows. Just like there is always another story just
waiting in the back of my mind.
You can read on to get a look at the books I have
already published and a bit of an explanation about
each. Thanks again and remember, a book is never
happy until it is read and loved by others.

The Novels

"Foretold" - Predictions come true as the ultimate showdown between good and evil begins. One place in Idaho is a shining light for those looking for hope.

"Voices" - A serial killer is murdering the down and out as the voices whisper. Sadly, even the killer can't remember the murders.

" Obligations" - A car wreck takes Josh to the other side and then back as he is given the obligation to find and destroy the evil that followed.

"Tunnels" - Nikki is called home when her father becomes sick. It's not until she gets there that she finds he caught the disease through the tunnels in a parallel world.

"Capernicious" - Sue and Cheryl have been friends a long time, now Sue is married and finds her husband changing after starting his new job at Capernicious academy. The two friends have to get together to figure out why.

"B.A. 47" -   An explosion next to a subdivision reveals a conspiracy and the witnesses in the neighborhood are in a race for their lives.

"Pacific Passage" - Winning a dream cruise, Bree takes her two best friends along. The nightmare begins when the cruise wrecks as it goes through a vortex.

"Suppression" - The actual true story of a man with a device that can end pollution and create cheap or free energy, guess who doesn't want that? Maybe it could be the government and their big oil backers.

"Lies in Shadows" - Lucretia was sheltered all her life, now with her parents dead, and a memory block crumbling, she is finding the horrific reasons why.

"Phases" - George is a nice guy, well, except that one night a month. Usually, he'd give you the shirt off his hairy back. Hopefully Jake can help George out.

"Mystic Valley" - If the government hid the paraphernalia from Area 51, you might find it in Mystic Valley

"The New Moon Killer" - Not all killers strike on the full moon. Becca and Tom are hunting one in the present while Becca heads to past lives through hypnosis to help with Chronic Pain

"Healings" - As a healer, Andrew has walked the earth since Biblical times. Meeting his soul mate might change all that.

"Superstition Canyon" - The Native Americans hid a relic years ago, now it has been found and the finder has to be stopped before he unleashes something terrible.

"Collisions" - Using a Ouija Board, Lindy causes a rip in the veil between worlds, now they are colliding.

"Viewings" - As a remote viewer, Greg has seen a lot of strange things, but what he finds in an old barn will amaze even him.

"At Hidden Lake" - Something is hidden at the lake, three friends are in danger when they uncover the hidden secrets from WW II and who was behind them.

"A Gradual Decline" - Serial killer Riley Jackson is going to be executed. Rick Holton has the exclusive story, but does he have too much empathy for the killer?

"Judgments" - A serial killer is committing gruesome crimes, who, how and why, may shock you.

"Of Jeebies and Journeys" - The Jeebies have stolen something from Ellie. Her husband Jed is going to journey to the other side to try and find her and give it back.

"Into The Doorways" - Terrene is a parallel world in trouble, they have opened the doorways to try and find a new home. Not as easy as it sounds.

"Correlations" - Lacey is going to find everything is related and will need help from this world and the next to stop the past that is haunting her.

"Whitmore Hills" - The psychiatric center houses those with mental problem, but they aren't the crazy ones.

"Transpirations" - Jess is a healer, but a fringe religious group is going to try and stop that as a conspiracy unfolds.

"Realities" - Sometimes the realities of life are not what we expect and may be more supernatural than real.

"Presence" - Andi Moore has a special gift, she can see spirits. As woman are abducted, Andi is asked to help. This is only the second time in her life she has come face to face with evil.

"Just Divine" - When two friends buy a coffee shop with a house attached, they are going to find a twisted mystery with a paranormal twist.

"Disturbance & Destruction" - The worst has happened, a man brought the world to destruction. Now it is 2047 and a few survivors that escaped to a parallel world are headed back to search for any survivors and to see if anything of the old world is left.

"Deadly Afflictions" - Dealing with anxiety, Amy wants to change her life, instead she lands in the middle of murder, mystery and more.

"Fatal Pretense" - The people of Aurora were excited to have much needed jobs when a drug company opened its' doors. Then strange happenings and deaths have them scrambling to find the truth, before more bodies pile up.

"Believing" - In a world of good and bad, some people are gathering and discovering they have special talents and gifts that are a bit supernatural and badly needed to make the world a better place for all.

"Unveilings" - Coming back from a near death experience and waking in the hospital was a miracle. When Tina realizes she also came back without the veil that hides this world from the next, her life changes forever.

"Scrutiny" – A missing doctor, concerned friends and a hospital up to some strange and illegal things. Who's watching who in this medical conspiracy thriller?

"Perdish Inn" – Two friends step into horror, supernatural and suspense when they step into Perdish Inn. Stepping out is going to be the hardest thing.

"Power and Pretense" – When the wrong man is elected, nothing feels right. When he belittles the intelligence agencies, including the FBI, how are they supposed to protect the man? Death threats against him, mean they have to.

"House of Lies" - After being laid off, Ray Larsen finds a dream job. He is ecstatic, that is, until things happen and make all he hoped for a nightmare.

"The Earth Watcher" - Before Covid-19 hit and then ran rampant around the world, people were watching earth. The story follows one of the watchers to find why they have decided to hold a vigil over this earth.

"Persistence" - Years from now, many things have changed, but a few haven't. New viruses come and go. Families change because of circumstances. Ethan and Abby are an example of that.

"Entries" - Nick Porter inherited his grandparents' small farm, he also inherited the troubles he has found under a shed on the property.

"Disruptions" - In life things happen that can change a person's perspective. Can the way people handle things, good and bad, change all they know and how they act?

"Plots and Premises" - Trying to grab the American dream to own a home, a place for family, The Warner's land instead in a deadly conspiracy.
Based on a true story.

"Midnight On Owl Mountain" - Owl Mountain has also been a strange place, full of secrets. Lights above the mountain during the four solstices of the year add to the mystery. Ben and Kyle are heading up, despite the danger to see if they can unlock the mysteries.

"Between" - Jack is a special person, a near death experience takes him to a place between worlds. After he is sent back, Jack has a special job that has him interacting with spirits between worlds.

Obligations Return - Eight years ago, Josh died. He traveled to
the other side and was sent back with an Obligation. His job
was t find the evil that followed and destroy it somehow. He
thought he was done with evil, but no, it is back.

Mammoth Cave - Three friends know all about the horrors that
have happened up at Mammoth cave. The stories go back to
when Native Americans were driven from the area. But what is
gossip and what is truth? And who will be the next to die?

Jen's Journey's - 3 book series

"Perspectives" Jen's Journeys – Book 1 -
Jen is a widow who feels her life has come to a stalemate. She
is looking for more and buying an RV, heads into adventure she
never expected.

"A Time of Thorns and Roses"
Jen's Journeys, book 2 -
Jen is back and once again the older woman is in big trouble.
All Jen wanted was to try and begin a new life after her
husband died. That isn't happening.

"Animalistic Behavior"
Jen's Journeys Book 3 -
Jen is headed to a zoo camping trip and taking her two
grandsons along. Big problem when a serial killer is on the
loose.

<u>Young Adult Series, adults can enjoy</u>

"Parallel Adventures 1 - Into the Caves" - When twins Jayden and Jenny step into the caves near their home, they discover the doorway to parallel worlds.

"Parallel Adventures 2 - Secrets Revealed" - The Parallel adventures continue. Jenny and Jayden are going to find amazing secrets about the past, present and future.

"Parallel Adventures 3 - Strange Happenings" - More adventures as the twins find the strange things going on and the people they are helping are themselves.

"Parallel Adventures 4 - Spooks and Spirits" - The twins are twenty and embarking on strange adventure as they find themselves headed into hell and back to maintain balance in all the worlds.

"Parallel Complete" - Now readers, young and old, can grab all four books in the parallel adventures series.

Short Story Collections

"Visitations" - Can others reach us after they pass on to the other side, you might be surprised.

"Heartfelts" - Life hands us hard things, poems and short stories tackle them with uplifting messages.

"Wings to Whispers" - A touch or a whisper may just be a loved one saying hello from the other side.

"Life Bridges" - In life we build bridges, three people fought prejudice to build the bridges of understanding that touch our lives.

"Tidbits and Treasures" - Poems, poems and more poems, plus a few insights added in.

"Hypnagogia" - Short stories that delve into the strange place between being awake and being asleep. It is also the place my stories actually come from.

Young Adult Short Stories adults can enjoy

"Stretched Stories" - Tall tales that can be enjoyed by all ages and great to share.

"Stretched Stories 2" - More tall tales, read them aloud with the ones you love.

Comic books for adults

"The Golden Years" - Humorous comics about growing old.

"The Golden Years 2" - More comics, no one wants to grow old, don't go gracefully, have fun.

<u>Books for Children</u>

"The Alphabet Book" - Preschool reader, learn the alphabet with happy rhymes

"The Number Book" - Preschool rhymes teach numbers with fun

"The Secret Life of Goats" - Fun early reader, rhyming tale about a family of goats and the secrets they keep.

"No, Jimmy, No" - Nobody wants to hear the word "No". Jimmy looks for a place without the word. Fun rhyming early reader.